THE STRANGER
AT MY SIDE

J. W. BECKER

Dedication

To Maureen who will never be a stranger at my side, but my sister. Thanks for all the encouragement.

Chapter 1

Allison stood in the doorway looking into the bedroom at the man. She watched him carefully, he groaned and moved to his left.

"Do you think Charlie will let me keep him?"

Brandon sighed. "He's a man, goofy; you just can't keep him like you would keep a lost puppy."

She looked at her brother and frowned. "But Charlie found him and I want to keep him."

"Don't be crazy, Boo." Brandon had been calling his six-year-old sister Boo since she was a year old. It was the first word that she had said and the name stuck. He looked over at Boo, she could be unreasonable and committed in her weird ideas and thoughts. Once she took a scissor and cut off most of her hair. She was forced to wear a hat for over a month and when he asked her why she did it, she said her hair made her head hot. Now she was being unreasonable about this man that Charlie had found.

Boo walked back over to the kitchen counter and leaned against it before continuing her argument. "I'm going to keep him. Charlie saved him, so I should be able to keep him."

Brandon eyed his little sister and placed a bowl of cereal on the bar next to her. She climbed up on the chair and sat with her legs folded underneath her. She looked back over her shoulder and watched the man, but he was now still and quiet.

"I'm going to look at him again."

"You need to leave that man alone and eat."

Boo got down from the high stool and went to the bedroom that was right off of the kitchen. She peeked into the doorway at the big man sleeping in the spare bedroom. He didn't move. There was a large bruise on his left cheek and he had a black eye. He also had a cut across his forehead.

"Do you think he's dead?" She whispered in her brother's direction.

He joined her at the doorway and looked at the man. "No, he's just hurt and needs to let his body rest some."

"How do you know that?"

"Charlie told me. Go finish your breakfast."

Boo stomped back over to the breakfast bar and crawled into the chair again. She played with her cereal rolling the milk around and watching little lumps sink to the bottom.

Brandon pointed at the bowl. "You better eat that and make sure you drink all of your milk because............"

Boo mumbled, "I know. You milked the cow just for me."

"Right. I'm going to feed old Jack before we go meet the school bus and you leave that man be."

"Yeah. Yeah."

Brandon yelled as he ran out the door. "Five minutes."

Boo concentrated on her bowl of cereal, she hated it, but oatmeal had to be cooked and it took too long. Brandon had been really careful yesterday not to burn her oatmeal so she felt obligated to eat it, but today was cold cereal. She just didn't like breakfast of any kind. She managed to choke down three more spoonful's of the cold cereal before she gave up.

She heard the man in the bedroom cough. Boo slid down from her chair and went over to get a glass of water; very carefully she carried it to the bedroom making sure that she didn't spill any of it. She stood next to the bed. The man suddenly opened his eyes and looked straight at her. She smiled.

"Hey. I'm Boo. You were coughing. I brought you some water."

She held up the glass so he could see it. The man nodded and Boo carefully climbed on the bed and held the glass to his lips. He drank eagerly until the glass was empty. She whispered. "Charlie said I'm not supposed to bother you."

"It's fine." He croaked.

"Charlie said you're supposed to sleep a lot, so close your eyes and after school when I come home, I'll read to you. Dillon is going to come to see you later."

"Who's Dillon?"

"He's, my friend. You got a name?"

"Morris."

"That your name?" Morris shook his head slightly. "Okay, Moose, you sleep well. I have to go to school. I'll see you later."

Boo ran out of the door and yelled bye to Moose. He chuckled; he thought that she had called him Moose. She ran to the barn and right into Brandon. "Did you feed old Jack?"

"Yeah," he said as he walked out of the barn. He doesn't look so good and he hardly ate anything. I have to remember to tell Charlie to look at him. Come on, or well be late for school."

"Who cares? Hey, the man waked up and his name is Moose."

~~~
~~~

Morris Allen Duffy knew he was hurt. He felt the pain go right through his head. Somehow, he had to find out where he was and how long he had been here. He didn't know what the hell had put him here. He wondered where here was. The last thing he remembered was a blinding light and an energy hit.

Morris had transported from his time, which was as far as he could figure, a few hundred years in the future, but nothing made much sense to him right now. He had an exact destination and it had been programmed in, he should be in the city of Atlanta, in the state of Georgia, but it seemed that he was on some rural farm. His head started to pound and he decided to let all the questions rest because there wasn't anyone here to answer them anyhow. Everything was extremely quiet so he knew he was alone. He wondered who the child was. He needed to look around and make sure that he wasn't in any immediate danger.

Morris pushed his big frame up into a sitting position and groaned. His head was pounding to a definite beat and it was intense. He ran his big hand through his thick black hair and felt a large lump behind his left ear. He had another one on the back of his head.

"Great. Guess that's why I can't think straight right now."

Morris was 6 foot five, his blue eyes were glazed over from the pain and he had to move slowly. He had a scar under his left eye. It happened in a drug sting. Drugs are still a problem hundreds of years in the future, but they seemed minor now. The knife cut under his eye had never healed properly and left a big scar. He had gotten used to it.

Morris pushed off the bed and found his legs shaking beneath him, so he moved even slower holding onto a dresser. He looked at his reflection in a mirror above the dresser and saw fever burning in those eyes that stared at back at him. There was a large bandage across his forehead with traces of blood on it; he gave a fleeing thought to pulling the bandage off but dizziness overtook him, and that was enough to stop him. He also had a black eye and a lot of facial bruising.

Morris swayed and quickly moved back to sit down on the bed as his legs began to buckle. He placed both hands against his head, moaned, and then collapsed back onto the bed. He looked out of the bedroom door and could see the kitchen beyond. It looked normal enough even though it appeared strange to him, but it appeared normal for this time that he was in now. He had studied many pictures of this time at the learning center. He knew he couldn't push himself any further right now, and he didn't have a sense of danger, so he closed his eyes and let sleep take him.

Chapter 2

Boo was standing next to Brandon at the end of the road where they get the bus for school. They were waiting under an old shade tree. He looked at his little sister and asked, "how do you know his name is Moose?"

"He told me." She said easing down to the ground. She pushed her chestnut brown hair out of her face and looked up at her brother. "I gave him a drink of water."

Boo's unruly hair blew gently in the breeze falling back into her face. Her green eyes flared at her brother as she tried to tie her shoe and then tugged at her dress. She hated that she had to wear a dress to school; her blue jeans were more comfortable.

"He said his head hurt so I told him to go back to sleep."

Brendan grabbed Boo's hand and helped her up. "We need to go home."

"Why?"

"Come on." He said and started the quarter mile walk back to the farmhouse. Boo looked up at Brandon, he had the same color hair, but his eyes were as blue as the sky above. At ten he was stocky, but not fat, just all muscle. It came from all the work he did around the farm and the constant time he spent on a horse. Someday Brandon would be as tall as Charlie, but much bigger in stature. Charlie was 6 foot and had the same color hair, but he sported blue/green eyes, sort of a combination of Brandon's and hers. Charlie was their older brother and at nineteen he had been taking care of them for almost a year.

They had spent a whole year apart from each other when their father died. It had been a terrible time for Boo. She had felt his loss and constantly was afraid after that. Charlie was only seventeen and they were all put in State Care until he reached the age of eighteen and fought to reunite them.

Dillon Bartlett, the town's doctor, and a personal friend of their late fathers had helped Jim Bowerman, their closest neighbor, convince Judge Landers to give Charlie a chance to reunite the family. At least that's what Boo thought had happened, but it didn't matter because they were all together again.

Boo thought that Dillon had to be the keeper of them because Judge Landers told him that he was responsible, but she wasn't sure what that meant either. Dillon had been a constant in their lives and even the year she spent in State Care, he was always there for her. She loved Dillon, he was her friend, and he always smelled good. He had fought the entire year to change their situation and ultimately Dillon and Charlie won in court.

The farm had been taken care of by their father's friend, Jim Bowerman; he ran their cattle over to his ranch and cared for them. He also made sure that the house was kept up until their return. He kept in touch with Charlie and made sure that the farm would stay in the Crawford name. Through Jim and Dillon's efforts they eventually got to go home and be together again.

Jim Bowerman was more than a neighbor; he was always considered a good friend and one of the few people Charlie allowed into their lives. Dillon was the only other person Charlie felt comfortable around. He had taken on the responsibility of both his brother and sister and never thought twice about it. Charlie loved Brandon and Boo and was grateful to both Jim and Dillon for their support.

While they were in State Care, Charlie spent more time at the farm then he did there. He would hike over and work all day long and sometimes he didn't return to the dorm home he was assigned to. He would stay in his own bedroom at the farm. They had shut off electricity and water, but he didn't care. Jim Bowerman did and got the utilities turned back on. The Sheriff, Andrew Towline, gave up trying to take him back, and the truth be told he often turned a blind eye to the entire situation. Luther Crawford had been a good friend of his also, and he liked his children. He felt they needed to be together.

~~~

Boo ran to keep up with Brandon. She was having a hard time and called to him, "slow down. Your legs are a lot longer than mine."

"Sorry, Boo." Brandon said. He eyed his sister critically; she was nine years old and rather small for her age. She always slowed him down, but he didn't want her to have to run to keep up, he slowed his pace. It didn't take them long to get back and as they slid under the fence their big black-and-white unknown mixed dog met them.

"Hello, Connery." Boo smiled and planted a kiss on the dog's nose.

"Boo, don't do that, it's nasty."

"Why?"

"Germs that's why."

"Who's got germs?"

"The dogs got germs."

She threw her arms around the dog's neck and said, "Connery don't have any germs. He's real clean."
~~~

They rounded the barn and headed back to the farmhouse. The blue/gray building always looked like it sighed as they approached it. The building was old and worn, but they kept it in decent repair which made all the difference.

Charlie, Brandon, and Boo were in the process of painting the house. It was something they had been doing for the last year. It had become a constant project, one that may never see an end. Charlie usually came home so tired at the end of the day that he didn't have the energy left for painting. Boo didn't think that they would ever get it done. She looked at the tree she had painted on the side of the house and grinned. It would make her sad when they painted over it, but at the rate they were going it would take a long time. The barn also need painting, but that was second to the house.

Boo ran up the six stairs and out of the Georgia heat. She sighed as she entered the coolness of the house. The first thing she did was kick off her shoes and wiggle her toes, she felt better already.

Brandon marched through the hall and into the kitchen. Boo followed him dropping her book bag between the hall and living room. There was only one bedroom downstairs, it had an attached bathroom, off the kitchen. This is where the man she considered her new friend was sleeping.

Charlie had found him half in, half out of Dawson's Creek. He was lying next to a big boulder that an oak tree had grown around. He was unconscious when he found him. Moose had blood all over his face. Carefully, Charlie walked over to the big man and leaned down to look into his face. He shook him, but he didn't move so he put his hand on the side of his face and talked to him. He went to the creek, took off his bandanna from around his neck and wet it. He knelt down next to the man and gently wiped his face with the bandanna. After a few trips to the creek, he managed to get most of the blood off of his face. He had a bad cut on his forehead that was still oozing blood.

Charlie sat down next to the man and waited, but when the sun started to dip over the hill, he knew that he had to do something because he just wasn't going to wake up on his own. He was big and he had a hard time getting him out of the creek.

Charlie looked down at the man. "I have to go, but I'll be back for you. I'll get my brother and he'll help me because you're too heavy for me to do this alone."

Charlie took one last look at the man and then ran back to the house. He was sorry that he hadn't ridden out instead of walking. He opened the front door and went up the stairs. He found Brandon in his room doing his homework.

Brandon looked up and asked, "where have you been? And why are you wet? I was about ready to come and look for you."

"There was a man in the creek, and you need to help me because he's wet and hurt. I can't deal with him by myself, he's too heavy. We have to hurry."

"Hold on. What man?"

"I don't know him. We need to get Jack and a rope.

Brendan followed Charlie into the barn. He told him to go get a blanket and the rope from the tack room and he would get Jack. He put a halter on the old horse and led him out of his stall. He threw the blanket over his back and lifted Brandon up. He handed him the rope and crawled up behind him. They rode down to the creek. The man hadn't moved. Charlie slid down then helped his brother. He stepped over to Moose, knelt down and looked at Brandon.

"He's awful big and we may not be able to get him up on Jack."

Charlie had been right; the man was extremely heavy. He took the blanket off of Jack and wrapped it around his withers and neck. Next, he placed the rope over him and put the other end under Moose. He placed the rope under the man's arms and across his chest tying it tightly. Charlie moved Jack forward while Brandon guided the man the rest of the way out of the creek.

"Okay, Brandon."

After getting the man completely out of the water they had the problem of getting him up on Jack. Brandon brought the horse over to Charlie and lined him up next to the man.

"Now what?"

"I guess we have to get him on top of Jack, but it isn't gonna be easy because he's so heavy. We may not be able to do it."

Just as he said it, the man groaned and started to stir. He was just conscious enough that he was able to help get himself up onto the horse. After five minutes of struggling, they managed to get him seated on Jack. Brandon covered the man with Jack's blanket and climbed up behind him. Charlie told him to hang onto to him.

~~~

Brandon looked at the man who was lying in the spare bedroom, he appeared to be sleeping.

"I think he sleeping. We missed the school bus. Charlie will be here in about fifteen minutes and he's going to be mad. How do I explain this?"

"I don't know. Maybe when my Moose wakes up, he can explain it."

"Don't call him that."

Boo shrugged. "But that's his name. He told me."
~~~

"First or last?"

"Maybe both. I don't know."

People don't have two names that are the same."

Charlie stood in the middle of the kitchen with his arms crossed. "Who has two names and why aren't you two in school?"

"My Moose waked up." Boo gave Charlie a little smile as she flung herself at him. He braced, caught her in his arms and lifted her up for a hug. He immediately lost his smile and adjusted his attitude to suit the situation. He looked sternly at his brother and sister.

Brandon frowned. "Here it comes."

"I will ask again, why aren't you both in school?"

"Because Moose waked up."

"Who's Moose?"

Boo pointed to the bed. "My Moose."

Charlie grinned at her, "he's Moose?"

Boo nodded her head, "yes, and he's mine."

"Give it up, Charlie." Brandon shrugged. "She doesn't make sense most of the time and who understands her anyhow. The stranger you found," he pointed at the bedroom like Boo had done. "That's Moose."

Boo fumed and stamped her foot, "that's his name."

"Yeah, anyhow Boo said he woke up so we came home."

Charlie turned to his little sister, "Boo."

"Honest, Charlie," she said crossing her heart. Moose waked up and I gave him water."

"Well, he's not awake now." Brandon said. "I looked."

Charlie took Boo's hand and went into the bedroom; he placed her in the rocking chair, next to the bed, before going over to put his hand lightly on the man's forehead.

He turned to his brother, "Brandon, go fetch a cool cloth for his head."

"Does he have a fever?" Boo asked, "is he going to die, Charlie? Like daddy did? Please, don't let my Moose die."

Charlie stopped with his hand in midair and went over to his little sister. He picked her up and sat down in the rocking chair with her.

"I don't think the man………"

"Moose, Charlie. His name is Moose."

"Okay. Moose. I don't think Moose is going to die and what happened to daddy was an accident. He fell and hit his head and just couldn't wake up."

She pointed to the bed. "Moose hit his head."

"But you said Moose woke up already."

Boo got more comfortable in Charlie's lap and thought for a moment. She looked over at Moose and smiled. "We have to take care of him. He's mine now."

Moose didn't move, he laid as still as possible because he wanted to observe his surroundings before he let anyone know that he was alert and conscious.

"Charlie, did God take daddy to his house?"

"Yes, daddy's in heaven."

"Why did he have to take him?"

"Because he probably needed someone special, someone like daddy."

"I wish he could've stayed here with us. I didn't get to member him before he went away. I hardly member what he looks like anymore."

"The word is remembered, and you do have a picture of him."

"He's been gone a long time."

Charlie leaned back and said quietly, "three years. Three long years."

Brandon came into the room and held up a cloth. "It's good and cold."

Charlie sat Boo back in the chair again and went over to Moose; he placed the cloth on his forehead and covered his eyes with it. "We need to let him rest and you two and I need to talk."

"Talk about what?" Boo wanted to know.

Charlie returned to the rocker and sat down pulling Boo back into his lap. "Sit down and make yourself comfortable, Brandon."

"Boo looked up at her brother and asked, "did I do something awful, Charlie?"

"No, but you have to quit claiming strays as yours."

"What's a stray?"

"All those animals you find. Like Connery for an example."

Boo gasped. "My Connery is not a stray. He's my best friend."

The big dog had followed them into the house and thumped his tail when he heard his name. "Well, I don't exactly mean Connery, but you can't carry everything you find home and claim it. All these hurt animals can't live here or soon we won't have room in the barn for the cow. There is one other thing, you have to do, and I want it done by the end of the week. No excuses why it will not be done."

Boo raised her eyebrows a little and her mouth went into a pout of anger. "What's that?"

"You have to release Molly."

"But, Charlie, she's......."

"She's all better and we talked about this before. You know this is not a place for a deer to live. She needs to be out in the forest with her own kind. She needs to be free. You do it, or I will."

Boo said sadly, "I'll do it. I'll give Molly back to the forest."

"That's my good kid. She'll be much happier there. And there will be no more ditching school for any reason. Do you both understand me?"

They answer together. "We understand."

Moose had been listening to their conversation. He wondered what a deer looked like.

~~~

Charlie sighed. "I guess were going to have to call the Sheriff."

Boo jumped up, "you're going to call the Sheriff on my Moose?"

"Maybe, but he's not hurting anything being here, so let's wait until he wakes up and find out who he is. Brandon, since you didn't make school today, we need to go move the cattle over to the South
~~~

pasture and then there's fencing to be mended. Get August and Joe. They're both good cutting horses."

"I'll go saddle them and meet you at the barn."

"Good, and you Miss Boo," Charlie picked her up and threw over his shoulder patting her butt. "Go make dinner, but no cooking. I don't want you to burn the house down."

"Aw, that was an accident."

"You're an accident waiting to happen, no stove. Make sandwiches and no peanut butter and jelly. Try ham and cheese."

"Okay, Charlie."

"You leave Moose sleep, if he wakes up, ring the bell."

~ ~ ~

The old house had a large wraparound porch that went from the front and over to both sides of the house. Outside the front door there was a large bell with a rawhide rope attached low enough so that Boo could reach it. When Luther and Grace Crawford had married, he installed the bell so she could ring it to call him if he was out in the pastures. It could be heard across the fields and had been used for all kinds of purposes, lunch, dinner, and emergencies.

It rang when Charlie had fallen out of the oak tree and broken his leg. Grace used it to call Luther when she had gone into labor with Boo. When she rang the bell, Luther had been working in the south pasture. He immediately jumped on August and rode up to the house where he found Grace collapsed on the front porch in a pool of blood. Luther placed her into the station wagon and headed for the Barry County Hospital where four-pound little Allison Ann Crawford was born. Grace never saw her daughter. The doctors had tried to stop the hemorrhaging, but she died on the operating table.

Charlie had been thirteen years old when he carried the baby into the house. Brandon had just turned four.

After Luther's wife died, he had to juggle caring for his children and running the farm. He kept Boo with him when the boys were in school. When Charlie came home, he took over making sure that his sister was well cared for.

Charlie made sure supper was on the table and took care of the house, when he had time, he would help with the cattle. When Brandon turned five, he was put in charge of milking the cow. He quickly learned how to take care of the horses too. Everything seemed to be going well until the day Luther died.

Charlie was graduating from high school the following week, he was seventeen years old, Brandon was eight, and little Boo was only four. Boo had been in the barn when Luther fell and she tried to help him, but he didn't answer her when she asked him what was wrong. She shook him and kept telling him to wake up. When she didn't get an answer, she ran to the front porch and rang the bell, but there was no one there to hear it. No one came.

The little girl went back to the barn and sat next to her father. She took his hand and held it; she cried begging him to answer her. Soon, she got tired and laid down against him and fell into a restless sleep.

It was almost dark when Charlie and Brandon arrived home that night. They had been at a graduation rehearsal which Brandon had stayed to watch. The Milton County school bus dropped them off at seven as the sun was setting.

Charlie knew something was wrong when he walked into the house and everything was dark. There wasn't a light on in the whole place. He switched on the lights as he walked through the entire house searching the downstairs. He called for his father and then Boo, a call that brought no response. He sprinted up the stairs to the second floor and checked the three bedrooms and two bathrooms up there, no one was there. He ran downstairs calling for Brandon.

Brandon got two flashlights from the downstairs pantry and they made their way down to the barn. It was almost dark; the lights hadn't been turned on so Charlie hit the switch inside the door. He heard Maybelle Blue, the cow, bellowing as he turned on the lights. In the middle of the barn, sitting on the floor, was Boo, rocking back and forth as she held her father's hand.

Charlie ran over and knelt down next to his father, there was blood on the floor under his head. Boo also was sitting in a pool of blood; it was on her face and hands. Charlie folded Boo into his arms and said, "Brandon, call the rescue unit."

Brandon ran back to the house and called 911. Miss Mary Marie Current, who was Tustin's town operator took the call. Her voice was quiet, but yet firm. "Just what kind of emergency do y'all have out there, Brandon?"

Brandon said as calmly as he could. "Daddy fell, and he's not moving, ma'am."

"I'll send Mike and Nate out there, honey. Y'all go back to the barn and keep your daddy quiet."

The Fire Rescue came quickly. Dr. Dillon Bartlett was at the fire department when the call came in and went with them. Within ten minutes they rolled up next to the barn. Charlie had Brandon milk the cow just to shut her up and keep him busy. He still had Boo secured on his lap, he kept asking her if she was hurt, but she wouldn't answer him. She sat quietly staring at her father.

Dillon was the one to tell Charlie that Luther had died. "I'm so sorry, Charlie. He probably died immediately."

He squatted down next to Boo, and when she didn't respond he took her from Charlie. He carried her over to the ambulance and after cleaning the blood off of her he determined that she was not physically injured, but she was unresponsive. He decided to take her into the hospital to be checked out. That was the day their life would change forever.

Chapter 3

Boo watched as Charlie and Brandon rode out, there were going to check and move the cattle. She was used to being left behind, but it still made her mad because she felt she could ride as good as, or even better than Brandon. Her horse, Buckles, was a great cutting horse and they worked well together. She shrugged and went back into the kitchen, got out a loaf of bread, and placed it on the counter. She was about to cut into the bread when a crashing sound came from Moose's bedroom. She ran over to find him sitting on the floor.

"Did you fall down, Moose?" She asked looking up into his face. He looked at her and shook his head. He leaned back and waited for the dizziness to stop, he felt like he would throw up.

Boo sat down next to him and asked, "are you okay? You want some water?"

"Do you have any Lonetall?"

Boo screwed up her face and whispered the word Lonetall to herself. She didn't know the word and wondered exactly what it meant. She thought maybe it was something to eat.

"Is that a sandwich?"

Moose looked at the sweet little girl sitting beside him and said, "no." He groaned. "It's medicine for my head to make it stop this damn pounding."

His head hurt so bad that he didn't feel like he could even lift it to look at her anymore. The dizziness had gotten worse when he tried to get up. Now just moving made his head pound. He fought the nausea that threatened him.

"I don't think I know what that is, Charlie will be back soon and maybe he'll know, and Dillon said he was coming tonight and he should know all that stuff. He's a doctor and really smart."

"A doctor?"

"He kind of looks after us, well, Charlie does mostly, but we need Dillon too. Charlie said you not supposed to move around and I'm not supposed to not pester you."

Moose opened one eye and looked at this skinny little kid next to him. She had one of the sweetest faces he had ever seen and she was smiling at him with bright green eyes that twinkled. He moved slightly to stop the ache in his back.

"It's okay, you're not pestering me. You think you can help me get up?"

"You kinda big, and I don't have Brandon help me, but I'll try. You want me to make you a sandwitch?"

"I believe the word is sandwich, and no thank you, my head is killing me so I'll just stay in bed for now and not move. When is this Dr. Dillon coming?"

"Sometime tonight. He can fix you really good. He fixed me when I got sick and wouldn't talk."

Moose screwed up his face and looked at the kid. "What's your name?"

"I'm Boo. Actually, my name is Allison Crawford, but everyone just calls me Boo. I told you before, don't you remember, Moose?"

"No. Do you know who I am Boo?"

Moose thought his name was actually Morris Duffy, but he wasn't sure about that and Boo kept calling him Moose, so maybe that was his name, but was that a first name, or last name?

"Sure, I know you, Moose," she said as she helped him back onto the bed and struggled to cover him with a blanket. She crawled up on the side of the bed next to him and sat cross legged.

"Charlie found you, but Brandon said I can't keep you because you aren't a puppy. He said if you didn't have a family then maybe I could keep you." She put her finger to her head and said, "at least that's what I think he said because maybe that's how it works. I found Connery and he didn't have family, so he's mine now. Dillon belongs to me too."

Moose closed his eyes as he listened to her rattle on. He didn't know what she was talking about, but she seemed to claim a lot of people as hers. Most of what she said didn't make sense to him. Charlie had found him and now she claimed him as hers. The big man laughed at the thought of this little girl placing her mark on him. He briefly wondered who Charlie, Brandon, and Connery were, but he let it slip from his mind because he would find out soon enough.

Boo patted Moose on the chest and slipped off the bed making herself comfortable in the rocker as she continued to talk to him. He tried to pay attention and listened carefully so he could learn more about his situation.

Boo went back over to the bed and crawled up next to Moose again. She looked carefully at him. He opened his eyes and winked at her. She giggled and leaned her head against his shoulder; he wrapped his big arm around her because he thought she needed comfort. As she snuggled next to him, she began talking about how her father had left her. How he had gone to heaven. She told him about the fall and the terrible hours she spent holding him while he died. Moose gathered her closer and nestled her against his chest. Boo found that she could hardly keep her eyes open and fell into a light sleep. He looked at the small child, she was so fragile and he felt bad that she had to live with this memory. She was also too trusting. She showed no fear of him. His own daughter would know better. He wondered if he should take away her bad memories and give her more peaceful thoughts, but no, it was part of her and as much as he would like to erase the bad memories, he hesitated. He realized that he couldn't remember how exactly that was done. He thought he could do it, but he also knew he shouldn't. He was still confused and had only a slight memory of who he actually was, but one thing he did know was that he didn't belong here. He belonged somewhere else. But where? His head started to ache with the pounding that returned. He held Boo closer because for some reason he felt she needed to be protected.

Boo woke when Connery jumped up onto the bed. She looked at Moose and smiled as she gently removed his arm and slipped out from his grasp. She hugged the dog and he obliged her with a face wash.

"Boo?"

"You okay, Moose?"

"I feel better." He said as he pushed himself into a seated position. She smiled and asked him if he had a dog.

"I don't know, but I don't think there are many dogs where I come from."

Boo gave him a funny look. "That must be a really sad place. You need a dog, they're all warm and fuzzy and nice to hug. I'll share Connery with you, that is, if Charlie lets me keep you."

Moose laughed and then immediately stopped. His head made him stop as it throbbed enough to bring tears to his eyes. Boo noticed that Moose had made a hurt face and got up. She went over to the bathroom and came back with a wet washcloth. She climbed on the bed and gently placed it on Moose's forehead. He had laid back down on the bed with his eyes closed and didn't bother to open them as he thanked her.

"I would make you some soup, but I'm not supposed to touch the stove. Charlie doesn't want me to burn the house down."

"That's probably a good thing." Moose chuckled. "And I'm not that hungry."

A voice called out as the back door opened. "Boo. Brandon."

"That's Dillon. I'll be right back." Boo said as she jumped down from the bed. Connery was already greeting the doctor as Boo threw herself into Dillon's arms. He put his bag down and caught the rushing little body to him.

He grinned at the little girl. "How's my favorite girl?" He asked as he kissed her cheek.

She hugged Dillon and laid quietly in his arms for a few minutes, she liked how he felt and smelled. She liked when he held her because he reminded her of her daddy. "I'm fine, and so is Connery, but my Moose is really sick, his head Booms when it moves. Her little face turned serious as she spoke at an almost near whisper. "You've got to fix him."

"Who's Moose? Take me to him?"

Dillon thought about Boo and what she may have found. Charlie hadn't said anything except he needed him to come to the house tonight. He thought back to the last time he was called out to the Crawford place. Boo had called his office saying that she had an emergency and he had rushed out to find a dying bunny she had found. The rabbit died and Boo was inconsolable. She had already named the damn thing and he had to help bury, Mr. Thomas Jefferson Crawford, a.k.a., bunny rabbit. They had placed flowers on his grave. After the burial, Dillon carried Boo over to the porch where he deposited himself in the rocker struggling her onto his lap. He let her cry and held her tightly in his arms. He hoped whatever Moose was it wouldn't die.

Dillon leaned down and took her hand. "Take me to your Moose." As an afterthought he hoped that she hadn't actually found a real Moose.

Dillon was surprised when Boo showed him the downstairs bedroom. There he found a man who definitely looked like he needed the help of a doctor. He went to work immediately assessing his injuries. Moose opened his eyes briefly and looked up at the man hovering over him. He decided that this must be the doctor.

Dillon needed to keep Boo busy, so he asked her to go and make him a sandwich while he took care of her friend. She said that she would make everyone sandwiches, ham and cheese. He said that would be fine, but as an afterthought called out to her. "No stove." He turned back to Moose and spoke in a deep quiet voice asking several questions. Moose kept his eyes closed, but answered the best he could.

When the doctor was done, he had sutured the deep cut across his forehead, bandaged his wounds, and gave him a tetanus shot. Moose had a black eye, and several contusions and abrasions all over his body. He looked like someone had taken a club and beaten him. Dillon was pretty sure he also had a concussion. He was preparing an injection of antibiotics when Boo walked in.

Boo walked over and stared in horror at the needle Dillon had in his hand. "You're going to hurt my Moose?"

Dillon turned around and smiled at her. "You know better than that." He gave Moose the injection and watched Boo screw up her face as if it was her, he was injecting. He went over and took her by the hand and directed her back into the kitchen. He pointed at the table, "finish the sandwiches."

Boo stomped over to the table, "fine."

She went back to making sandwiches, he went and opened the cabinet taking out a glass. He filled it with water and went back to Moose so he could help him take the medication that would ease the pain in his head.

"I want you to try and get some sleep. I'll be back in to check on you later. I have to go and make sure that Boo makes the sandwiches with ham and cheese and doesn't add peanut butter."

Moose chuckled, the little he knew about Boo, he was sure that was exactly what she would do. Dillon strolled into the kitchen, sat at the table and watched as Boo took out the peanut butter. He suggested to her that not every sandwich needed to be graced with peanut butter and maybe the ham and cheese should be just that, ham and cheese. She put the knife down and thought before agreeing with him. Dillon got up, got two glasses and filled them with milk. He placed several plates on the table, went to the refrigerator and took out peaches and cottage cheese.

Dr. Dillon Bartlett was no stranger to this kitchen, he knew it well, he had helped Luke and Grace Crawford rebuild and remodel this home. They had been married for three years when he first met them. Dillon had just lost his own wife, Christina, three months before when she died in an auto accident. The driver that hit her was a sixteen-year-old boy who was drunk at the wheel. He survived and served a prison sentence for manslaughter. Stanley Aston went to juvenile court and then jail for the accident that killed Dillon's wife. He was released six years later, got drunk again and ran down eighty-three-year-old woman coming home from Siler's market. The boy was in trouble since he was ten years old and at the ripe old age of twenty-four, he would spend the rest of his adult life in prison.

Luther Crawford had helped Dillon when he needed it most. Grace had taken him into their family. The 5-foot woman envelope him into her special kind of love and made him a part of everything. He was included in everything that was happening in their lives. He had been there for Brandon and Boo's birth, and he cried with Luther when he had to tell him Grace didn't survive Boo's birth. He looked over at the little girl; she looked just like her mother, the same small frame and fiery spirit. She had the same coloring and eyes that smiled at everyone. Dillon had seen the children through various illnesses including Brandon's pneumonia that almost killed him. He was also there the night that Luther died.

Dillon thought back to that night. He had been at the firehouse when the call came in; he was giving a refresher course to the paramedics in advanced life support. When the call came in, he jumped into the ambulance and rode along. When they got to the farm, they found Luther dead with little Boo sitting next to him. He didn't want her to see her father put into a body bag and took her to the ambulance, he held her all the way to the hospital speaking quietly to her. She never said a word.

Dillon tried to prevent the children from falling into the system, but Judge Neely wouldn't give him custody stating that he was not a married man and she could not in all good conscience award him custody of three children. She also thought that his schedule was too unpredictable and he could be called away at any time and the children would be left alone. Dillon fought for over six months and finally went to another judge he knew, Morton Silverman to intervene. In Family Court, District 110, he won temporary custody until Charlie would turn eighteen. He took the three children back to their home, the only one that they had ever known. He moved in with them. It was a month before he got Boo to come back to them; she hadn't spoken in all that time. He spent every minute he could with her.

Dillon had showered her with attention and love. He worked with her every day until she eventually started to talk, and now she was almost like her old self. She still had periods when she would get quiet, it was something he understood. He missed his wife as much as Boo missed her father. He would wait for her to come back to him, and then he would hold her and they would sit together quietly. Sometimes that was enough; sometimes she could not be consoled and wouldn't be able to sleep. That was when he gave her a mild sedative to help and, in a few days, she seemed to bounce back to normal.

When Charlie turned eighteen, he wanted to care for his brother and sister alone. Dillon wasn't happy about leaving, but he wanted to give Charlie his space and it seemed important to him. He didn't go far and kept a close eye on all of them. He still had a room at the farm and spent many nights there. This gave Charlie the independence he needed and made Dillon feel more comfortable about leaving the children alone, and now there was a man named Moose. He would again explain to Boo that she couldn't claim people and keep them. He also explained that she couldn't keep bringing wild animals' home, animals that she didn't seem to fear.

The problem was she collected them, but this was the first time she claimed a man.

Dillon was concerned because no one knew who he was, or where he had come from. He didn't have any identification on him and Dillon didn't like this whole situation. The man claimed he couldn't remember anything. He would also talk to Charlie about leaving her alone with Moose. He decided it was time to stay at the ranch for a while.

Chapter 4

"Dillon, are you listening to me?" Boo stood with her little hands on her hips looking up at the doctor.

Dillon who stood 6 foot four and weighed around 200 pounds smiled back at her. His deep brown eyes looked down at her as he pushed brown hair back out of them. He seriously needed to take some time and get a haircut.

He smiled again and then said, "sorry, Boo."

"Is my Moose okay now? Did you fix him?"

"I think we need to sit down and talk about this."

Dillon took her over to the front porch and sat down on one of the rockers. Boo pushed his arm away and crawled into his lap. After she was finished making herself comfortable, Dillon leaned back and explained in very simple terms about Moose's injuries. He wanted to make sure that she understood that while Moose was hurt, he would recover, but it would take time and care.

Boo thought about it very carefully and said, "I'll take care of my Moose." She had been relieved that Dillon said he would be all right.

"If we give Moose a little time, he should be fine. I'm hungry, how about you?"

"I'm starved."

Dillon took her hand and they went into the kitchen. He turned the burner on the stove and reach for a pot. Charlie walked in and went directly over to him.

"You've got a call. I caught it on the barn phone. They're going to transfer it up here. I'll do the soup."

Dillon took a good look at Charlie, the kid looked tired. He handed him the pot and walked over to his office to take the call. Charlie opened the can of soup and dropped it into the pot. He turned to Boo and grinned, "you stay away from the stove."

"Yeah, yeah, I know."

Moose felt better, but he was still in bed; he heard people talking and decided it was time for him to get up. He had to know what was going on. He slowly made his way into the kitchen and over to the stove to watch what was going on. He had seen something like this in his time at the House of Memory, but didn't exactly know how it worked. He reached out to the flame and Boo screamed.

"Moose. No!"

Charlie turned just in time to see Boo grab Moose's arm and jerked it away from the flame. "Why did you do that?"

"I've never seen it before."

"Seen what?"

"The fire. Is it hot?"

"Of course, it's hot." Charlie said giving Moose an unbelievable look. *How could he not know that fire was hot?* "Just what planet are you from?"

"Here of course. Earth."

~ ~ ~

In Moose's time, which was in the future about five hundred years, there was a great evil movement that was descending on the planet. Actually, descending on what was left of earth.

Moose belong to the Arctic League of Law Enforcement whose sole responsibility was to bring this evil under control and to justice. He was an important part of the control group in the team; there were only sixteen of them left. Collectively, they were attempting to apprehend all of the remaining criminals. At this point there were only six of those left, but they were all deadly. The battle had gone on for years.

He ticked off the names of his head of those who were left.

Raymond Bing, male, age 44

TaLana Allen, female, age 32

Tanocka Burns, male, age 42

Jackson Raymond Garcia, male, age 32

Peter Ripken Ray, male, age 57

Chan Dana Ray, female, age 22

Peter Ripken Ray was the father of Chan Dana Ray. The father/daughter team had wreaked havoc on the planet. They were as deadly as poisonous snakes. Peter Ripken Ray was now dead. He had been searched out by the Baker team. There were four of them, and unfortunately in the apprehension of Peter Ripken Ray two agents, Malcolm Nobles and Benjamin Lassiter were killed. It had been a great blow to the team.

Peter Ripken Ray's daughter, Chan Dana Ray, who is also known as Landa Masta, disappeared in the confusion. At this time her whereabouts were unknown and she was actively being sought.

Raymond Bing was on the planet Digger Too. Digger Too had been discovered approximately a hundred years ago and colonized shortly after. The planet was only 700,000 miles away from Earth and enjoyed the same atmosphere. It had four seasons and the sun shined almost all year. Even in the rainy season the sun shined. It was something that took getting used to. There were beautiful sunsets of various colors depending on the time of the year. Moose had always liked the magenta skies the best and he knew that one day he would go back there, maybe even to retire.

Digger Too had dark rich soil and can grow just about anything you planted. It was a quiet planet with a small population. Now, it had a killer on it. Agent Burke Margate was close behind Raymond Bing. He was determined to catch him and eliminate him.

TaLana Allen fled to the other side of a blue planet called Tiran. She was actively being pursued by agent Mark Kona Lester. Tiran was a mining planet that had been discovered as recently as seventy years ago. It had all the minerals and elements that were essential to the survival of earth, and it had also been colonized. The men who worked on this planet were rough and the few women that were there tended to their needs. The planet was dark and it seemed to have a perpetual haze across it. It was not a very inviting place to be, but this was where TaLana fled to, on the deserted side that was harsh and cold. The temperature could get below zero at night. There was some question as to whether or not she had survived.

Tanocka Burns was still out there in the unknown, but agent Johnny Donya was on his trail. He had been sighted on Earth, so it was assumed that he had stayed there and had not fled too somewhere else.

Morris was assigned to find Jackson Raymond Garcia. In the one working laboratory left they discovered that Jackson had returned to this time. The year was 1986.

Moose couldn't trust that Jackson wouldn't destroy this planet and then transported to another. It was inconceivable that it should happen. To destroy this planet was to destroy his planet, Earth, his home. He had to located and secure Jackson before it was too late, he had to find out exactly why he came here in this time period.

Time travel was strictly prohibited by the League. The only exception, and that had to go through the console of the league for time travel consideration, you had to exhibit extreme consequences were about to happen. There had been a whole debate on whether or not to abolish the method of future time travel. Morris thought they should destroy it.

Leonard Copinski was responsible for time travel; he had discovered how to accomplish it. In Moose's century he was considered what people of this time of 1986, would call a nerd. He had an IQ of over 260 which put him in the super-genius category. He had discovered time travel and said it was a snap, but he also warned it could be a deadly thing. Moose had gotten to 1986 in less than five minutes.

Moose knew that he had to save the people of this time to save his own future. So much destruction had already happened that would take a long time before things could be rebuilt and put right. When he left, Jackson and his associates had killed 90% of the population. Jackson had formulated a poison and injected it into the Earth's atmosphere. It was instantly lethal and only a small portion of the earth's population was left, that was all that had survived the attack. Moose was one of the soldiers that survived. LaBo poisoning was quick and efficient and there was no known cure.

Moose still didn't know how Jackson managed to bypass all the safeguards and get into the laboratory. It was the one secure place that had been left. Once Jackson got into the lab, he stole the device that they called the 'sundowner'. It was no bigger than a matchbook and it had given him the ability to travel unrestricted through time. There were only four that were known in existence. Jackson had one, and he had the other. He was unsure of who else had acquired the remaining two sundowners. He found it hard to believe that Jackson had gone rogue.

Moose had been hunting Jackson for a long time. Almost a year had gone by in 1986 standards. Jackson had stolen over six million Consul credits, but that was for his time of 2480. He didn't believe that they could be used here. The credits were not the only reason why Moose was hunting him.

Moose didn't understand how Jackson thought the Consul credits would be useful here in Earth's past. He read up on this time before he left and knew that they used conventional money. Perhaps he thought he could trade them.

Moose had seen pictures of money. He spent weeks listening to speaking tapes to learn about 1986. In his time, conventional money didn't exist except in the House of Memories. In the House of Memories, he had learned from the speaking tapes about money, but had never seen money.

He also learned that the House of Memories in his time was equal to the museums of this time. He would like to go see a museum because they revealed the secrets of the past. He was suddenly very tired and wanted to rest his mind so he went back into the bedroom and lay down. He wouldn't be finding Jackson today.

What Moose didn't know was that Jackson was innocent. He was not responsible for the poison, or injecting it into the earth's population. He was as committed to saving the earth as Moose was.

Chapter 5

Boo walked into the bedroom and whispered, "Moose. You want crackers with you soup?"

Moose sat up and smiled at her. "Yes, thank you that would be good."

Moose had no idea what soup and crackers tasted like because he got his nutrition from a liquid he consumed daily. It was called 'Semiliquid' and came in different colors. Each color was designated to a taste, but he didn't remember anything that was called soup and crackers. There were actually eight choices and he preferred the blue/purple ones which were made of some kind of berry extract. The liquid provided everything that was needed nutritionally and to continue a man's life source.

Brandon and Dillon came in and sat down at the table. Moose joined them and looked down at the bowl in front of him. He was surprised by the steam and the smell that was coming from it. He didn't realize that food of this time had a smell to it. It was something that he found quite intriguing. He wasn't sure how to continue so he watched as Boo picked up her spoon and dipped it into the liquid before she ate it. He picked up the spoon next to his bowl, it felt awkward in his hand, but he believed he could handle it. He watched her dip her spoon into the soup three or four times before he was willing to give it a try. He picked up a cracker and ate it before he was ready to do the soup thing.

"Is there something wrong with the soup?" Dillon asked. "You need to eat it because you need something in your stomach."

Moose eyed the spoon again; he decided that he had no choice but to attempt to eat the soup with it. He managed to get the spoon to his mouth without dropping the liquid all over. He couldn't believe how delicious this hot liquid was, it had something in it that was absolutely wonderful. He held up the piece of chicken from the soup. "What is this?"

Brandon looked at the piece of chicken on his spoon. "It's chicken."

"Chicken? This is the most wonderful thing I've ever eaten."

Charlie laughed. "You don't get out much, do you?"

Dillon had been studying Moose. There was something off about him. He didn't seem to even know what chicken soup was, or how to eat it. He decided that since Moose was going to stay here for a while, so would he. The man was strange, but he couldn't put him out since he was injured. Dillon would contact the Sheriff tomorrow and see if he could figure out exactly who this mysterious Mr. Morris Duffy was, and in the meantime, he would just keep an eye on him.

~ ~ ~

Jackson Raymond Garcia stretched. He pushed his shaggy hair back out of his eyes. He was thirty-two years old, but today he felt around eighty. He was stiff from sleeping on the ground. There was a time when he used to love to go to Cold Shiver Campgrounds, but that was when he was a kid and sleeping on the ground had been fun. It wasn't fun anymore and it didn't work for him. Tonight, he would have to find a hostile unit to rent. He disliked the small 6 x 6 rooms that were designated only for sleeping. They weren't comfortable and you are allowed to use them for only an eight-hour period.

"No. They are not called hostile units here." He thought for a moment and came up with the correct word. "I believe they are called motel rooms."

Jackson knew that he would have to acquire something called money from this time. He'd seen it a long time ago when he was a boy and his mother had taken them to the House of Memory. The question was where did he get it. He had credits from his time, but they wouldn't work here. He discovered that when he tried to use them at what he thought was a local eatery, but turned out to be a small store of some kind, the man had asked him if it was monopoly money. He had no clue what monopoly money was and left immediately.

Jackson looked down the road and decided he would have to walk until he found an establishment of some kind. He went west on Vermont Way which led him into a town called Naper. The first thing he came to was some type of store called 'All Things Great and Small'. He could see things through the window and wanted to check the place out; he followed several people into the store. He walked slowly and watched everything around him. For the next hour he just walked around and examined different items that were offered by the store. Some of the items were actually familiar to him, some of them seemed familiar, and some of them, he had no idea what they were. He was fascinated by the number of items in one small location. There were more things in this building than he had ever seen in his entire life. He walked up and watched the people who were paying with money that they had taken out of their pockets. After they handed the money to the other person, they acquired the products that they had selected. They put them in some type of bag and left with them.

Jackson wondered where they got this money. He left the store and continue to walk west on Vermont Way until he came to a smaller store, 'The Convenient.' He looked through the window and saw that there were only two people inside. He took out a device he had brought with him and held it in his hand. It was called a 'blanker'. With it he had the ability to immobilize a person for about five minutes. When they came back, they wouldn't remember a thing. As he walked into the store, he hoped that it had survived the transportation impact. A few minutes later he walked out the store with $420 and wondered if it was a lot of money. He knew it was stealing but there was no choice.

Jackson had actually arrived in this time after Moose, a week or so, and four days before the woman called Chan Dana Ray. Chan Dana Ray was directly responsible for the death of the entire community of, 'Rise Wells'. She and her father, Peter Ripken Ray had been responsible for the death of 60,000 people who lived there. She poisoned the water supply system and then put the blame on him. That was one of the reasons why he was being sought by Morris.

Jackson and Chan Dana had history together, he had fallen in love with her when she was only eighteen and he was twenty-eight. They had lived together for over a year before he discovered her true identity. She disappeared on the day he discovered the deception. He had known her as Landa Masta. It was the name she had used almost her entire life, but she was actually a daughter of one of the most famous criminals of their time, Peter Ripken Ray. Peter had been described as a criminal in the eyes of God and man. He was guilty of mass murders that had only been equaled in history to Adolf Hitler.

While Chan Dana had been responsible for the murder of 60,000 people, her father, Peter, orchestrated the mass murder of 90% of the world's population. It had a devastating effect on earth. The 10% that managed to survive were people who had gone underground. They gathered in the tubes that shuttled people from one country to another, but even this wasn't enough. They had lost people to disease and starvation before the air became clear enough for them to breathe it again.

Peter developed a gas called, 'Zena Vons', and he released it into the atmosphere. The weather was driven by air pressures called Blue Tear Waves. The Blue Tear Waves traveled on jet streams which directed the flow over the entire planet. The iconic part was that Blue Tear Wave was a natural global weather event that happened only every twenty-two years. They had planned well so that the entire planet would experience the weather phenomena and the Zena Vons gas that Peter had created. Clouds turned to sickly orange/green color and rained down with their deadly poisons. It lasted for three days and when it was done everyone who had been above ground died. After the three-day rains came another thirty-two days and thirty-two nights of death followed as the poison moved relentlessly on the wind patterns. Peter had planned very, very carefully, but he had made one mistake. One that allowed Peter Ripken Ray to be captured, tried, and then executed. No one knew why he had developed and released this evil into the world and he went to his death without saying a word. The devastation was as bad as the world wars that the earth had experienced hundreds of years ago, possibly worse.

In the end the dead had to be burned because there just weren't enough people left to bury them. After that, the rebuilding came as people sought out each other. They came together from other communities and bonded. It took over a year to establish five new communities, but this time they were all within close proximity of each other. That was all that was left with the exception of a few scattered people that would come at intervals and join them.

Chan Dana Ray had discovered one of the new communities and destroyed it before she jump time and ran into the past. She had sought revenge for her father's death.

Chan Dana Ray had left Jackson's 'Con-Red' identification card at the site to be found by the investigation squad. Since there were only fifty members left of that squad and it took an extensive time to do the investigation. As soon as Jackson had the opportunity to jump time, he did, now he would find Chan Dana Ray.

It was determined by the consul that Jackson had no culpability in the crime because he had a steadfast alibi, but some still condemned him and did not believe that he was innocent. He had been freed and vowed that he would find the person responsible.

Jackson has been in a medical unit having his liver repaired after Chan Dana Ray stabbed him while he was sleeping, she had left him for dead. His alibi was unshakeable. It was fortunate that a friend of his had come by to visit and found him or he might not have recovered. Once he did recover from his wound, he vowed that he was going after her and bring her back to justice. Unfortunately, Moose was unaware of Jackson's innocence and was tracking his old friend.

Jackson had gone back to his laboratory and discovered that Chan Dana Ray had been there before him, he knew it had to be her when he discovered one of his time transporters missing. The one that had been taken by Morris was accounted for, but there were at least three others. Chan Dana Ray had attempted to destroy the others, but failed in her attempt. He looked carefully at the one she had broken and realized that he could reconstruct the broken part, and then he went after her.

After Jackson fixed the remaining time transporter, he tracked Chan Dana to the year of 1986 on old earth. It had been pure luck that he managed to leave his time with the repaired transporter before anyone could stop him.

Jackson was going after Chan Dana and realized that he had to find her at all costs, she was a vicious serial killer. He wanted to bring her back alive, but knew that may be impossible. He wondered if he could actually pull a trigger on her, if he could kill her. He knew that if it came to that there would be no choice. He put the thoughts out of his mind.

Instead, he thought about his old friend, Bill Trader, who was now known as Morris Duffy. They had a long history together; he had met him when they were just children and they bonded immediately. They had become best friends, it was Bill who consoled him when his wife, Margaret died. It's been such a freak thing, one that he still didn't understand today.

Margaret had gone to see a friend of hers, Ella Martinez. She had taken a transport at the Antalya station and walked right into a drug sting. The Marshals were having a shootout with the Papuans gang. The Papuans had vowed to kill every Marshal they could before they took them down. The Papuan gang numbered seventeen. The Marshals, thirty-four. The gunfire took place on the platform of the Antalya station and when it was over, all seventeen of the Papuan gang lay dead. Four Marshals also were killed. Margaret was killed in the crossfire.

Jackson had been with Bill when his wife of seven years died of leukemia leaving him with a six-year-old daughter named, Kara. The two events took place within six months of each other.

He wondered how far behind him Morris was. He laughed, "Bill, I just can't get used to calling you Morris."

Chapter 6

"Hey." Dillon said as he placed a kiss on Boo's cheek.

"Are you hungry, Dillon?"

"Yes, but I'll make the lunch." He grabbed up Boo and swung her around. "That way we don't have to eat peanut butter in everything again."

When Moose heard voices in the kitchen he got up and went out to join them. He still felt shaky, but better than he had yesterday.

When Boo saw him, she yelled. "Hey, Moose, how are you feeling?"

"I feel much better."

"No headache, or dizziness? Double vision?"

"No, Doctor, in fact I have some of my memory back. My name is indeed Morris. When I told Boo my name, she thought I said Moose."

Boo looked at Moose and giggled, "Moose is much better than Morris, so I think we should keep it."

Brandon came into the kitchen and yelled. "Hey, y'all, I heard were going to have a real lunch for a change. I'm going to run out to the barn and milk Mabel, I'll collect some eggs too. Be right back."

"Please, sit down, Moose. Can you remember anything about what happened to you?"

Moose knew that he had to be careful in his answers. "My head still hurts." He said eyeing the doctor, "and I'm still tired. I'm afraid I don't remember too much." Dillon walked over and sat in the chair opposite Moose. Dillon pulled Boo onto his lap and planted a kiss on her head. He studied the big man carefully, his speech was much better, not so confused.

"You'll need to rest. Rest is the key word to healing here."

"Dillon," Boo said. "I was going to make soup, but Moose doesn't know how to work the stove and I'm not supposed to touch it. I guess that leaves us with sandwiches."

Dillon looked over at Moose suspiciously and wondered for the third time why he didn't know how to work a stove. He leaned down and said to Boo, "I'm glad you remembered about the stove. I'll cook. How about scrambled eggs? It's better for you than the cold cereal you've been eating for lunch." He turned to Moose, "do you have a last name?"

Moose wasn't sure if he had already told him his last name so he decided to be evasive. "I don't remember it because everything still is somewhat foggy. I'm actually glad I can remember my first name."

"So, you still don't know your name for sure? Do you know where you live? Anything about your life at all?"

"Not much. I do know that my name is Morris, where I come from, or where I was going is a complete mystery to me."

"You're pretty calm for someone who's disappeared from himself."

Moose decided he had to give the doctor some type of story so he said; "I think I was here in some kind of business."

"You know what kind of business?"

Moose frowned, shrugged and said, "I'm afraid not."

"Well, let's not push it. You had a bad concussion and should probably be in the hospital with it, but I didn't want to move you at the time."

"I think I'll be okay. I just need a few more days and I'm sure everything will come back to me."

Dillon was looking carefully in Moose's eyes. They were clear and except for the memory loss he was alert and could answer questions, so is mind seemed to be intact.

"You think you can eat some eggs for lunch? I can make them fried or scrambled."

Brandon bounced into the kitchen and held up a bucket. "Fresh from the chicken." He held up another bucket, "and the cow."

After lunch Moose went back to bed. He lay there for a while and thought about the eggs he had eaten; they were beyond delicious and something he had never had before. He suspected that there would be a lot of things that he had never tasted or seen before in this time.

Charlie and Brandon went out to the south pasture and Boo decided to watch some television. The doctor went on a call. Moose thought about television, he knew the concept of it, but had never seen it and wondered if he should get up and venture into the living room. He decided he was too tired and television would have to wait.

Several hours later, Dillon came back and called out to Boo. She came running from the living room. "How would you like a snack together?"

While they were eating their cake, Connery came over and nudged Boo with his large wet nose. She looked down at him and put her little hand against his forehead and started scratching. He nudged her again.

"He's hungry. I gotta go feed him."

"Let's do it together. Where are your brothers?"

"Cattle wrangling. They're moving them over to the South because the suns warmer and there's more grass over there."

"Let's go feed Connery."

After the dog was fed and the table set, Dillon went to check on Moose. While he was examining Moose, he heard Charlie and Brandon come through the back door.

"Hey, Doc." Charlie called out as he bound up the stairs. Brandon dragged in behind him and follow Charlie upstairs. Twenty minutes later both of them came down free of cattle dust. They were both hungry.

Brandon saw the pie of sandwiches on the table and eyed them with suspicion. "You didn't lace them with peanut butter, did you?"

Boo placed her hands on her hips, "No. Dillon wouldn't let me"

"Three cheers for the Doc." Brandon said. "You know she put peanut butter in our milk once."

"I was making a peanut butter float, and I didn't forget to put in the ice cream."

"Yeah, good thing we have a cow or we would've actually had to drink that stuff." Brandon said as he cautiously opened his sandwich to check its contents.

Dillon turned his attention to Charlie and asked what he knew about Moose.

"Not much. I found him down by the water and he was hurt, so I called you. Boo is the only one who talk to him at length and she told us that his name was Moose. She also said she's going to keep him."

"Okay, I'm definitely going to call the Sheriff out to see if we can identify him because all he seems to remember is his first name, or maybe it's his last. He doesn't seem to know exactly who he is."

"How can it be, Dillon?"

"The concussion maybe. All he claims to remember is waking up here, but I don't think our friend in there isn't telling us everything. Charlie, I don't think you should leave Boo alone with Moose."

"Why?"

Dillon shook his head, "I thought Boo was the only one who was naïve. We don't know this man and she's just a little girl."

"We're never gone long and I have work to do on the ranch. Boo can take care of herself. She can be quite resourceful if she has to be, and there's the bell if she gets in trouble. He's been here for four days and nothing's happened."

"Until we figure all this out, I'm staying here."

~~~

The next time Moose woke up the house was quiet. He lay very still and waited, just listening. Five minutes later he sat up. He was grateful that his head now aloud it and didn't pound so hard. Whatever the doctor had given him helped tremendously and he actually felt better, not great, but better. He touched his injured arm and that was also better. He decided it was time to try and get out of this bed for more than a few minutes, besides he needed to
~~~

answer natures call. Very carefully, he eased out of bed and happily his legs decided to hold him all the way to the bathroom. After that he took a few more shaky steps and went into the kitchen. The bright sunlight streamed through the window and over the sink. He stood there for a few minutes just enjoying its warmth. The sun seemed to be so much warmer in this time. He heard something and turned around, Boo standing in the doorway, once again with her hands were on her hips, she was grinning.

"Hey, Moose. You all better now?"

"I do feel much better."

He sat down at the kitchen table. He looked around and was charmed by this farmhouse kitchen. He felt like he didn't belong here although everything seemed somewhat familiar. Moose got up and savored the warm feeling surrounding them. He felt a peace filtered through him. He ran his hand over the smooth kitchen counter and looked at the small stained-glass train that adorned the window. There was a tiny engine, three cars, and a caboose all in bright colors of red, green, blue, and yellow. There were small touches of the family that lived here throughout the kitchen. He admired all of it as he looked around. A stuffed rag doll with a ragged blue dress sat next to the sink. There was a model plane lying on the counter next to the coffee pot, and hanging on a double rack next to the door, a rifle. It was an ancient rifle, one that he had seen in The House of Memories, but he thought for this time it was brand new. There was a desk in the corner with several Books that lay open as if someone had been interruptible studying them. A crayon drawing lay next to the Books. It looked a little like Connery.

"Where's Brandon?"

"He went with Charlie to Mr. Taylor's. I think Charlie's going to sell some of our cattle. I'll make you something to eat, but I can't use the stove. Remember?"

"Something about burning the house down?"

"Yeah. Charlie says I'm not big enough, and I did sort of start a fire once."

"I think I understand."

"You're big, and you can use the stove."

Moose again looked at the stove that he had seen only once before when it was actually burning with fire. He still had no idea how to make it work. Where he came from, they no longer use stoves, if any existed. He thought about the food he ate and how it was provided, they use dispensers. It was all terribly efficient. He was about to ask Boo how you turned it on when he remembered something. It came back to him in a flash. There was information left back by that stream where Charlie had found him, information that couldn't fall into anyone else's hands, information that could wreak havoc on this world. He also had several other devices that he had brought with him. They were all back at that stream. He had to go and retrieve them before someone else found them.

"Boo, can you take me to the spot where Charlie found me?"

"Sure, but what about eating?"

Moose looked at the stove again and said, "I think we should stick to cereal."

Boo was interrupted by the slam of the side door. Dillon stood just inside the kitchen door frowning at Moose. He had gone on a house call and tried not to be gone too long because he still considered Moose a stranger, and he wasn't sure he trusted him, not yet.

"I guess you're feeling better. How are you today?"

"You're right, Doctor, I do feel well."

"Good, because the Sheriff's coming out to talk to you later."

51

Chapter 7

While they were having dinner the phone rang. Boo got up and answered it. She giggled. "Hey, Sheriff, how are you?"

"Just fine, Miss Boo. Can I speak to Doc? Is he there?"

Boo giggled again. "Yes, sir. Hold on." She held up the telephone. "Dillon, the Sheriff is wanting to talk to you."

Dillon took the phone from Boo. "Run and finish your supper. Hey, Andy."

"Doc, I got your call. Do you have some kind of trouble out there?"

"Not really, at least I don't think so. I do have a patient who can't remember who he is. All we know for sure is that his first name is Morris."

"Where'd you find him?"

"Charlie found him down by the stream that runs through their property. He was half in and half out."

"You don't recognize him?"

"No, sir. I thought it would be a good idea if you came out here and had a look. We're trying to convince Boo that she can't keep him."

The Sheriff laughed. "That child. Somehow every stray in the county Boo fines. I'll be over in a little while."

"Appreciated it."

The Sheriff arrived an hour later. He brought Deputy Kevin Waters with him.

Charlie opened the door. "Andy. Kevin, come on in."

The three men shook hands. "Good to see you again. How's everything going?"

"Good, I just sold some cattle and we're going to build a new chicken coop."

"Chicken coop?"

"Brandon has a passion for them and wants to breed them. He wants to buy Australorp chickens. He wants to give them a try and it will bring in good money. He claims that they will improve production."

"Never hurts to give it a try, but what exactly are Australorp chickens?"

"They're pretty easy going and friendly, black in color and their eggs are light brown. They can lay approximately two hundred and fifty eggs a year. They're real good nesters and mothers. Their affordable and pretty much a peaceful bird. They also make sweet soft clucking sounds."

The Sheriff chuckled. "I can't wait to meet these birds."

The Sheriff shook hands with Dillon and offered his to Moose. Moose had watched carefully the way the two men greeted each other and took the Sheriff's hand.

"Let's go into the living room." Charlie said. "It's a lot more comfortable in there."

They all sat down, Boo went over to sit next to Moose. He smiled at her and put his arm around her. The Sheriff cleared his throat and looked over at Moose. He was a big man and stood at least 5 inches taller than him. His blue eyes contrasted with his dark black hair; he still wore a bandage across his forehead.

"Doc here has filled me in on your condition. Can you tell me if you remember anything, like your name?"

"All I remember is the name Morris. I don't know if that's a first name or last name."

"You're sure that's the only name you can remember?"

"Yes."

"Do you know where you live?"

"No. The first thing I remember is waking up here."

"Doc said you were here for business. What exactly does that mean?"

"I really don't know. It was just a thought I had."

"Do you have family in Tustin? Or anywhere else in Georgia?"

Moose shook his head. "I have no idea."

"Okay, here's what we're going to do. I'm going to take a picture of you and take your fingerprints. If you have any criminal activity it will turn up in our system. If that doesn't work, we can circulate your picture throughout Georgia."

Boo jumped up and blurted out, "my Moose is not a criminal. He never."

"Now, Miss Boo, we're just trying to find out who he is and this is one of the ways we can do that."

"Charlie."

"It won't hurt, Boo, and maybe we'll find out who Moose is and then he'll know too."

Boo turned to the Sheriff and asked, "you promise me you won't hurt my Moose?"

"Have you ever known me to hurt anyone?"

Boo thought for a moment and then said, "no, Sheriff, I reckon not."

Moose knew his fingerprints wouldn't show up in this time. They would find nothing on him so he didn't object to the Sheriff printing him. There would be no record for him anywhere in the 1986's.

Moose was photographed, printed, and questioned again. The Sheriff was going to put his fingerprints in the AFIS (automatic fingerprint identification system)

Sheriff Townley called Dillon two days later with his findings. "Am I disturbing you, Doc?"

Dillon sat back in his recliner and put his feet up, he kicked off his shoes. He was comfortable in his office and one of his comforts was this recliner. He had bought it right after he moved in. When he had a long day, it was a welcomed relief to lean back in it.

"You're not disturbing me, I just finished office hours. What did you find out about our mystery man?"

"Nothing. Absolutely nothing. He's clean. He is nowhere in our system. I couldn't even find someone slightly matching his description. I'm afraid that until he remembers who he is and where he belongs there isn't much we can do. He's not wanted for anything and didn't hit the system at all."

"I guess we'll just have to wait."

"I'm still going to play our wild card and distribute his picture to all the Sheriff's departments in Georgia."

"Thanks, Andy, I appreciate it. Call me if you find out anything."

"Will do. Later, Doc."

Dillon closed his eyes and leaned back as he thought about the man called Moose. There were so many unanswered questions about him, and to his way of thinking, it was not only about his identity.

Why didn't the man know about fire? If Boo hadn't stopped him, he would've placed his hand right into it. The stove seemed puzzle him and he had no clue how to use it. When the telephone rang it startled him. He looked at it like it was a wild animal. Dillon had watched closely as he picked the phone up and placed it to his ear, and started to talk. It also seemed to puzzle him.

When Boo introduced Moose to her pony, Buckles, he stared at her like he had never seen a horse before. He stood looking at Buckles for a full ten minutes before he approached her. Very gently, he ran his hand over her back. He grinned and lightly touched the horse's head. Buckles leaned into Moose and almost sighed with the pleasure of his touch.

Dillon was really surprised when Moose wrapped his arms around the pony's neck and held her tightly to him. The softness of the pony seemed to fascinate him as he rubbed his hands up and down her neck. Simple things around him not only surprised him, but he found delight in them. Even the flowers that grew wild in the pasture seemed to be strange to him. He picked up a flower and felt it, and then smelled it. His eyes lit up with pleasure. Could this man have never seen a flower before? That was highly unlikely. There were so many things that seem foreign to him, but they were very common things that they saw every day.

Chapter 8

When Moose woke the next morning, everything was extremely quiet around him. He rolled over and found a note from Boo.

The note read:

Dear Moose,

I had to go to school. I will be back at 2 o'clock. I left you a sandwich in the refrigerator. You have to pull the refrigerator handle out to you to get it to open. It's easy. See you when I come home.

Boo

Moose listened, but heard nothing. Charlie was probably out in the pasture somewhere; Boo and Brandon were at school. The Doc probably went off to the hospital which meant that he was totally alone. He got up and was surprised how good he actually felt. He still had a slight headache, but that could be dealt with.

He decided to have a look around, so far, he had been only in the peripheral areas, the kitchen, and the family room. The bedroom he was in had two windows across from the bed. It also had an attached bathroom with a shower, sink, and a small closet. He opened the door to the closet and found towels, wash rags, and various items that he couldn't identify.

Moose went into the kitchen and saw a large glass rabbit on the counter. It was filled with what he thought were cookies. He opened it, took out one of the round discs and smelled it. Cautiously, he took a bite. He couldn't help but grin, he took the cookie and moved over to the box in the corner. He had heard Charlie call it a refrigerator. Boo said there were sandwiches inside. Carefully, as instructed by Boo, he yanked on the door and it opened, to his surprise a light went on.

Inside the box were all kinds of food items. This was real food, not the liquids he was used to. He picked up an orange and examined it closely. He smelled it and then took a bite. It squirted out from where he had broken open the skin on the orange. He couldn't believe how it tasted.

"This is wonderful, I think I'm going to like real food."

He took the orange with him and went into the family room where he sat down on a long couch that took up the entire wall. He's stared at the square box across from him. He had seen Charlie use it, but wasn't sure how to make it talk. He stood in front of it for a long time before he remembered that Boo called it a television. He went back and slowly sat back down onto the couch. "Now just how would you work a television?"

He looked down at the small table in front of him. He picked up the Book that Boo had been working in. The front of it said it was a coloring book. She had been coloring in it with various crayons that were in a box next to it. He leafed through the coloring Book and smiled; the children of this time wouldn't recognize what a coloring book was.

A loud noise came from the front of the house, he got up and went to investigate it. Boo's dog, Connery, followed him outside. Standing next to the porch was an animal he had never seen before. He stared at it and it stared back at him. The goat bleated at him.

Moose looked from the goat to Connery who seemed unconcerned about this little brown and white animal. Moose slowly sat down on the porch step and stared at the goat. In the future animals were not a common site. He was seeing this one for the first time.

Moose had gone, in his time, to the 'House of the Past', and sat in a darkened room where images of things that no longer existed, or were slowly declining, were projected. He thought he remembered seeing an animal similar to this one, but he couldn't remember what it was called or what its purpose was.

After studying the goat for a while, he held out his hand. The little goat moved forward and sniffed it and then pushed his nose into Moose's hand. It felt soft and warm. He grinned, "that nose of yours is wet and cold."

He slowly reached out to touch the soft fur of the goat. He tentatively touched both the white and the brown spots to see if they would feel different. They weren't any different.

"That's Alfred." Boo said as she put her books down next to Moose. "He supposed to be in the pasture, but he always manages to get out."

"Alfred." Moose chuckled. "What exactly is an Alfred?"

"He's a goat, don't you know what goat is?"

"I've never seen one before and I didn't know what it was called."

Boo sat down next to Moose. "How come you don't know about goats, or things like stoves?"

"Where I come from there are no such things."

"Don't you have any animal friends?"

"There are very few animals and those that are around are kept in a special place to preserve them. There are groups trying to save what's left. They've had some success, but no one is allowed to see the animals."

Boo shook her head. "That's just sad. You must live in a very awful place. I don't think I'd want to live there."

Moose looked down at Boo. She was so innocent compared to the children of his time, "I agree with you."

Moose picked up one of Boo's school books. This was something they also didn't have in his time. Everything was done by air reading. All you did was think of what you wanted to know, press a corner button and that activated the image. It appeared in the air before you. He looked down at the book, turned it over, and asked, "what is this?"

"It's my reader. It has stories in it."

Moose held the book and turned it over several times in his hands. He carefully opened it and moved through the pages. "What a wonderful thing to have."

"Oh, the book belongs to the school and they just lent it to me, but I have some books of my own. Charlie said you can learn anything from books."

"Do you think I could see them?"

Boo didn't know why Moose would want to see something like a collection of books, but she didn't have a problem showing them to him. "Sure, come on."

Boo and Moose spent the next hour looking through her small library of books. She watched him as he carefully went through each book looking at the pictures and reading the captions underneath. He seemed to be delighted with every book he picked up.

"If we can get a ride, we could go to the library. They have a lot more books than me."

"Is that where they house the books?"

"That's where they keep a lot of them, but I guess housing them would be the same thing. Moose, you say you live here, but you don't know anything, why not?"

Moose looked at this little girl and tried to decide if it would be a smart thing to tell her exactly why he didn't know about things in the century, he would have to tell her some of the things about his life.

"Boo, can you keep a secret?"

Boo crossed her heart. "Yes, I can."

"Okay, here it goes. I live here on earth, but at a different time."

Boo screwed up her face and asked, "how exactly does that work?"

"I'm from the future. Your future. My time, is hundreds of years from now. I was sent back here by the League."

Boo put her arm around Connery, "how can you do that? What's the Leak?"

"It's League. It's a group of people, law people like your Sheriff. In my time, traveling from there to here is possible."

"Okay, if you say so. Why did you come here?"

"I'm looking for a man, his name is Jackson Ramon Garcia. He came back here from my time and I have to find him before he does irreparable damage."

Boo screwed up her face again, "I don't think I know what you just said."

"Sorry. Jackson may do something in this time that I can't fix."

"Oh, okay." Boo said not really understanding what he meant. "Maybe you can tell the Sheriff about Jackson and that he is missing, and he can help you find him."

Moose slowly shook his head, "no, I think it's better to leave the Sheriff out of this. He might not understand. Boo, I need to go back to where your brother found me."

"Okay, we have to ride over there because it's kind of far. I'll get Joe because my Buckles is too small for you."

They went to the barn to get Joe. She didn't really understand everything that Moose had said to her, but he was her friend and in need of help, so she would help him. She brought Joe out of the barn and over to the corral fence. She had a bridle in her hand. Moose had no idea what the thing was and he was surprised when she yanked on the horse's mane and he lowered his head. He watched in fascination as this small child handled the huge horse with ease. He had to admit that he was leery of the big animal, but she showed no fear at all. He watched carefully as she expertly placed the bit into Joe's mouth and then threw the reins over his head.

"I can't saddle Joe because it's too heavy for me. Do you know how to saddle a horse?"

"I never saw a saddle."

"Come on, I'll show you."

They went into the barn and Boo pointed to Joe's saddle that had been thrown over his stall fence. Moose walked over and touched it, and then he spent a few minutes just studying it. He turned to Boo. "How does it work?"

"I guess we better take my saddle blanket instead."

They went back out to Joe; Moose had the saddle blanket in his hand and stared at it. Joe turned around to look at him, he asked, "You won't bite me, will you?"

"Joe don't bite. Just throw it over his back, he's too tall for me to do it." Moose threw the saddle blanket over Joe's back, and Boo gathered the cinch, walked under the horse and buckled it on the other side.

"Are you sure we can't walk?"

"It would take a long time and Charlie would be mad if I'm not home for dinner."

Boo took Joe over to the corral fence and slipped onto his back. She looked down at Moose, "get on the fence, and then just slide up on behind me."

"Are you sure he won't mind?"

"It's okay, he can carry both of us easy."

Moose was finally on Joe, Boo moved him out slowly. It didn't take long before Moose felt comfortable on top of the horse and actually was enjoying the gentle sway. He laughed.

"What's wrong?"

"Nothing. I would never be able to do this in my time."

"Why not?"

"Because we don't have horses. Well, actually we do, but they're protected and not available to the general population."

Boo turned slightly to Moose. It was hard for her to believe everything he was telling her. "That's just horrible. Why don't y'all have horses?"

"I guess because it's a whole different world that I live in."

"I don't think I'd like it there."

Moose didn't want to tell Boo about how dark the future was going to be. Most of the animals had died in the first wave of the destruction. He didn't want to tell her about the devastation and how most of the population of earth was eliminated. He didn't know if the protectors were actually still alive. She was just a little girl and didn't need to know any of this.

He thought about the protectors, they were responsible for all the animals that were left and the variety of plants that were abundant in this time of 1986. Most of what he saw here was gone. There was no way of knowing how much, if any of them had survived.

The world that he lived in was definitely different from this one, they were struggling to save what little was left. They would have to repopulate the earth with not only people, but animals and plants.

The thought that Jackson Raymond Garcia and Chan Dana Ray, or Landa Masta, as she was also known, could do to this time what had happened in his world was unconscionable. He could find no reason for it except that these two were bat-shit crazy. He shook his head when he thought of his friend, Jackson, it was hard to believe he was a part of this. He knew that he had to stop them at all costs. He hoped it wouldn't be his life. He knew that he shouldn't be putting Boo in this position, but it was the only person he felt he could trust, even if she was a child. He would protect her with his life, and hope that that would be enough.

Chapter 9

When they got back to where Charlie found Moose, she pointed to her left at a rock formation next to the river. "I think that's where you were, over there in the water."

"Let's go have a look."

Moose slipped down from Joe's back and then went to help Boo down, but she had already grabbed Joe's mane and let herself down. He stared at her, "that's amazing."

"What's amazing?"

He pointed to the horse, "how you get down from him."

"Joe's too tall for me to just jump down, so I have to kinda ease off of him."

"Doesn't he care? Doesn't that hurt when you pull on his hair?"

"No, and it's called his mane, it's the only way I can get down. Come on, I'll show you where Charlie found you." She dropped Joe's reins and motioned for Moose to follow her.

"Wait. Won't Joe run away?"

Boo looked over at Joe. "No, he'll just stay there and eat the grass."

"Eat what?"

"Grass. Horses eat grass, hay, oats and they love sugar cubes."

"Are you sure? I don't think I can walk all the way back."

"I'm positive. Come on."

Moose looked around the area, it was mostly trees, grass, rocks, and a swift running river. "Did Charlie find anything besides me?"

"Like what?"

"I had a bag with me. I really need that bag."

"I don't know, maybe it got in the water."

Moose looked at the rapidly moving water. If it did fall in, he knew that he would never find it, and that meant he may never get to go back to his own time.

Moose and Boo looked all around the surrounding area; he was just about to give up when she called to him. In her hand, she held up a small blue bag. He grinned, "where did you find it?"

"Under the ledge over there. If it wasn't blue, I might not have found it. The color is why I saw it. It kinda called out to me, if you know what I mean."

Moose opened the bag; everything was in there including his transporter. He was so happy that he picked up Boo and swung her around. She giggled wildly.

"We should go back. I'm getting really tired and we don't want Charlie to get mad at you."

Moose lifted Boo up onto Joe's back, and then he got up behind her. The ride back was pleasant, but when they rode up, Dillon was waiting for them.

"Hey, Dillon." She shouted.

"Where have you two been?"

Boo slipped down from Joe; Moose followed close behind her. "Me and Moose went for a ride over to the river."

"It's late, you need to get ready for dinner. I'll take care of Joe."

After Boo left, Dillon turned to Moose. "You can't take off with her like that. She's not supposed to leave the farmhouse area when no one else is here. We want to know where she is at all times."

"Sorry, I didn't know."

"Boo is just a child and she doesn't have a good sense of danger; I don't want her to get in trouble because of that. The day Charlie found you she was supposed to be home, not riding alone, that's how Charlie found you. He was looking for Boo. There's also been a mountain lion spotted around here, in our area. Right now, it's dangerous out there."

Moose had no idea what a mountain lion was, but by Dillon's tone and he suspected that it was actually a dangerous animal of some kind. "It won't happen again. In fact, I will probably be leaving here in the next few days. I've recovered enough physically so that it won't be a problem, and hopefully the rest will come back to me with time.

~~~

Sheriff Towlend called Barry County Hospital and had Dillon paged. He waited patiently the few minutes it took for him to answer. "Dr. Bartlett."

"Dillon, Andy Towlend, can you drop by the Sheriff's office on your way home?"

"Sure, what's going on?"

"Well, sir, we need to discuss your friend, Morris Duffy."

"Moose? Did you find out who he is?"
~~~

"Come by after you're done."

"Give me an hour."

Dillon walked into the Tustin Sheriff's office as the sun was beginning to set. It had taken him a lot longer at the hospital because he had an emergency before he left. Everyone knew the Doc; Deputy Kevin Waters shook hands with him.

"How are you, Doc?

"Good. How's the family?"

"Okay. Jake is growing like a weed; can't believe he's going to be three this next week."

"They don't stay little for long."

While Dillon was talking to Deputy Waters, he looked around the Sheriff's office. It'd been quite some time since he had been in here. There were three, small prisoner cells across the room with a gate separating them from the other half of the office. On the other side of the room there was a desk where Kevin sat, a couple of file cabinets, and a telephone on the desk. Across from the entrance the door there was a corridor with two offices in the back. One was used to store supplies; it included a safe. They also kept all their weapons and ammunition back there, and across from that was a room where Sheriff Towlend had his office.

Dillon was on the Town Console, he had to speak to them about either moving the Sheriff's office to a larger facility, or adding onto the building. There was adequate land for that to happen. There just didn't seem to be enough room for them to work efficiently.

Granted, Tustin was not a hot bed of crime, but the office area was definitely cramped. There were stacks of paper all over because there was nowhere to put them.

"Dillon, come on in."

Dillon walked in and smiled at his old friend. Andy gestured to the chair across from his desk. He sat down and tried to make himself comfortable, but found it was almost impossible.

"You need a new chair, Andy, this is uncomfortable at best."

"I've been meaning to get one. Here," he threw Dillon a cushion to put on the chair seat. "Reason I asked you to come here is because I've been making inquiries about your friend out there."

"What did you find out?"

"Well, sir, it seems like he doesn't even exist. Morris Duffy is a ghost. His fingerprints are nowhere in the system, his face is not recognized in the system either, and I made inquiries all the way to Chicago. Nothing. It's like he popped out of nowhere, a ghost we call them. He has no Social Security number, no work history, no known family, or friends. There is not one person who can come forward and say that they know this man."

"There has to be some paper trail, everyone has one."

"That's not always true." Andy got up and picked up a folder that was lying on the file cabinet behind him. He opened it, "he has no driver's license, car, or credit cards. No address. He doesn't even have a damn debit card. Does he still claim that all he can remember is his name?"

"He says it's a total blank."

"What do you think, Doc?"

Dillon leaned back in the chair and quickly thought better of it and sat forward. "He does know his name, but claims he knows little else about his life. It's called retrograde amnesia; in other words, he has forgotten his entire past. Moose did have a blow to his head and he had vomiting and fatigue afterwards. He could have a brain injury, but when I suggested he go to Atlanta to have a scan, he refused.

At this point, he has memory loss and doesn't even know simple facts about his life. All his life experiences are gone from him. He doesn't remember past events. And he seems confused about commonplace things in our life. He doesn't even know how to use the stove."

"Will his memories come back?"

"It's hard to predict, Moose is unaware of what we consider even the common things in life. He understands the spoken word and can read the written word, but things like the kitchen stove and fire are a mystery to him. He almost put his hand in the fire on the stove, Boo stopped him. When Connery came into the room, he didn't seem to know what a dog was. Things that we take for granted are confusing to him. He doesn't seem to be disorientated, so I'm not sure what's going on."

"Unless he remembers something we may never find out the true story of who he is."

"He told me yesterday that he's going to leave in a few days. I don't think he has any kind of a plan, or really knows where he'll go, but I'm sort of glad that he's going to leave. Somethings not right about him, something is strange, but I don't think is dangerous."

Chapter 10

Jackson was walking through the Atlanta underground. It was 12 acres of land with three levels that offered shopping, restaurants, and entertainment. It was also a place he had effectively gotten lost in. He discovered there was an entire second floor section that was vacant. No one seemed to come up there, or even care about it. He spent the last month being invisible up there.

Back in the day, after it was created, in the early 1970s, the underground was considered a hotspot for nightlife in downtown Atlanta area. It was popular because alcohol was so easy. At the time, Fulton County was very relaxed in their alcohol consumption laws. Today, it was being considered for renovation to make room for apartments, office spaces, shopping, and even more restaurants, but in the meantime, it was a great place to disappear in. No one would be looking for anyone there.

Jackson knew that Bill Trader, (Morris Duffy) the man that Boo called, Moose, was somewhere close. Jackson knew that Moose would have to follow him, and would eventually trace him. He was good at his job.

Jackson knew that Moose was in a town called Tustin, Georgia. He would need to get there, and find him first. He was desperate to find his friend, he needed to convince him to team up with him so they could go after Chan Dana Ray together. It was a big gamble, but one that Jackson was willing to try.

Jackson pocketed his blank timer device; he may need it again. With it he could immobilize someone for five minutes and they would have no memory of it. It was a perfect device. The only problem with the blanker was the side effects. Headaches, nausea, but that didn't last long. He decided he would only use it if necessary.

Jackson held the Sundowner in his hand. It was the most important thing he had and he had to find a secure place for it. No one could find it because this was the only way he could get back to his own time. Like Moose, it allowed him to travel through time.

Jackson, searched for days before he was satisfied that he had found a safe place for the Sundowner. The abandoned restaurant had an attached space which he had made into a living space for himself, it was quite comfortable.

In the kitchen area behind the refrigerator, he discovered a panel and opened it. He wasn't sure, but he thought it was some type of electrical box. He would not have found this space except he needed to hook up the refrigerator to use it. He had gone to a secondhand Bookstore and searched for something that would tell him how to use a refrigerator. He learned that it was simple, it just had to be plugged in.

The old Bookstore was right in the underground. He didn't have to buy the Book because a man behind the counter named, Dude, that was what he called himself, saw him leafing through the Book and asked if he needed help. Dude laughed when he showed him how to plug in the refrigerator.

Jackson carefully placed the Sundowner inside the panel and then sealed it before pushing the refrigerator back into place. Now it was time to wait. Once the underground stores shut down, He went to work. He carefully selected the store that he would enter. It was called 'Stanley's way'. Opening the door was child's play to him and only took a few minutes. He cautiously entered the store. He was there to take only what he needed.

He started with the clothing area and secured several pairs of pants, four shirts, socks, and a pair of Boots. As he was going to the back of the store he spotted a leather coat, he took it, found a green canvas bag and loaded everything into it. He continued to walk around the store until he came across an area that had weapons. These were not familiar weapons to him, but he needed something. He went around the counter and to the back where a rack of rifles and pistols were displayed. He did recognize them as weapons, and stood there for a long time just studying them. He wondered how they actually worked. He looked at the lock on the cabinet and smiled, he had it open in a minute. He took down one of the rifles and placed it on the counter, he also took several of the revolvers.

Jackson was about to leave when he remembered that rifles and pistols needed something called bullets. He rummaged through some of the drawers and the cabinets until he found them. He would take them back to his temporary home and study how to use them.

The man he had met in the book store was named, Nate Omron. He was seventeen years old and lived in Atlanta. He had been a great source of information, he was the man called, Dude. He decided to contact him and ask him about the rifles and handguns. He was the only person he had actually spoken to since he had been here. He arranged a meeting with him.

The Dude was sitting on the outside of a restaurant called, 'The Green Onion.' When Jackson was walking towards him, he was suddenly confronted by three teenagers. They had purposely bumped into him.

"Guy's, please, just go about your business, and I will also."

"We would," the kid called Tuff McGuire said. "But we need some money, and you look like you want to give us some, so you're our business."

"Look," Jackson said. "I don't have any money. I'm flat broke."

"You don't look like you're broke, man." Acer Flynn sneered as he moved behind Jackson.

"I don't want to hurt you, boy, so just back off."

"Will you just listen to him?" Laughed Larry Keystone. "Big talker. Give us your money, or you'll be the one who's hurt."

They had started to circle Jackson who stood calmly waiting for their next move.

The Dude had seen what was going on and slipped off the bar stool he had been sitting on. He moved up behind Acer and pressed his knife into his back.

"One wrong move and you die. Leave the man alone, call off your wolves."

Dude had run-ins with these three before. They had come into the store he worked for and tried to steal merchandise. He ran them out and warned them to never to come back.

"We'll get you, Dude you want to be dead?"

"Wrong answer." He said and press the knife a little harder into his back.

Acer got the message. "Back off. This asshole will cut me."

"In a heartbeat. This here is a friend of mine, a really good friend. Now, take your little Gang Banger friends and split, or would you rather be the one who is dead? I got nothing to lose by killing you."

Acer moved quickly away from Dude. "We're out of here." When he got a distance away, he turned and yelled, "you're dead, Dude. We'll get you."

Jackson was watching everything that went down. He would've intervened if things had gotten out of hand, but he had sized up Acer and his friends, they were cowards with big mouths.

He walked over to Dude. "Thanks."

"My pleasure. Those punks are wannabes. Not one of them will make it to 16. They're too stupid and will get themselves killed."

Jackson sat down at the table across from Dude. He took a sip of something called a Coke that was placed in front of him. He looked at the glass "that's really good."

"Coke is always good, better with a cheeseburger. The waitress placed a plate with a cheeseburger and fries in front of Jackson.

He pointed to it. "Cheeseburger?"

"Man, where do you come from that you don't know what a cheeseburger and a Coke are?"

Jackson realized he was tired and leaned back in the chair. "It's a long, long way from here, Dude."

Jackson made a quick decision, one that he hoped wouldn't come back to haunt them. He needed Dude, the big question was, how much should he tell him.

"I need help, Dude. Your help, but you have to know that it could be dangerous."

Dude got a wide smile. "Bring it on."

Jackson told Dude that he was staying on the second floor in the underground.

"Cool."

"We need to go back there. I have some things that are not familiar to me and need to know how to work with them."

Dude had no idea what Jackson was talking about, but he liked the man, he was strange, and somewhat of an outcast, but very likable. Hell, he was an outcast, and this man was somehow special, he just knew it. He could feel it and strangely enough he did want to help him.

"Let's go. If it's as easy as the refrigerator, it will be no problem."

Jackson led Dude up the back way to the second floor. They went through a doorway that opened into another room.

"Hey, I didn't know this was here. It must've been something the workman put up so that they could disappear and take a nap or something."

Dude slowly walked around what could pass as a small apartment. He stopped at the refrigerator and laughed.

"Let's go in the back room." Jackson said as he led the way. On the table the rifle and pistol sat. He pointed to them. "I need to know how they work."

Dude walked over to the table and picked up the rifle. He had grown up in a very rural area and was familiar with all types of weapons. He carefully placed the rifle down and examined the pistols. When he was done, he turned to Jackson, "these are fine weapons. Did you steal them?"

Jackson hesitated for half a second before he answered, "yes."

"Well, you're a thief, but an honest one, if there is such a thing. I can show you how to use them. What are you fixing to do with these, save the world or something?"

"I hope so." Jackson said quietly.

Dude studied him for several minutes and wondered what he got himself into.

Chapter 11

Boo and Brandon were sitting on the front porch with Dillon, Charlie, and Moose. Moose was slowly rocking back and forth in an old oak rocker that Luther had made. He couldn't believe how wonderful it felt to just sit and relax. It was something he hadn't done in so long he almost forgot how. The weather was pleasant, and cool. They had just finished supper. Steak, corn on the cob, mashed potatoes and gravy. Moose also drank a large glass of milk that came from the cow. He was becoming very fond of that cow.

It was quiet, restful, and he savored it. He knew he was going to leave soon because he had to find Jackson. Jackson and Chan Dana, who was the worst one? Who should he go after first?

Moose was pulled away from his thoughts. "Moose," Boo said shaking his arm. "Can you remember where your home is yet?"

"I can remember a little. Where I came from is far from here."

"I know that, you already told me. Would it take a very long time to get there?"

"Pretty long."

"Charlie said you're a stranger and I shouldn't talk to strangers. I don't think you're a stranger, you're my friend. I wouldn't walk with a stranger at my side, only my friends."

Moose completely forgot about the others. He pulled Boo close and held her securely in his embrace.

"We will always be friends and I'll never be a stranger to you, or you to me. All of you have saved me, and I'm going to try to save all of you."

"What does that mean?"

Moose was about to answer when he realized the others were listening. He smiled and said, "Nothing. Nothing to worry that pretty little head of yours about."

~~~

Charlie was worried about Moose. The man seemed troubled and he knew all about that. He had plenty of troubles in his life. He was still struggling every day just to keep things stable. He always had Brandon and Boo to take care of, and the ranch to run. There were times when he wondered if he could go on, times when he wanted to give up, but something inside of him always stopped him. He had faith in the land, and his little brother, who always helped him. Even Boo tried to help.

Brandon would work until he was so tired, he could hardly walk. Charlie wanted more than that for him. And Boo, sweet, trusting Boo who collected strays, strays like Moose. He would work the ranch until he dropped if he could keep them all together.

Now, he had to decide what to do about Moose. It was time to find out exactly what he was going to do. There was something seriously wrong about him, but he wasn't sure what that was. Dillon felt it, and asked the Sheriff for help, but the Sheriff didn't find any information on Moose. He called Moose a shadow, ghost, he came from no place and as far as anyone could tell, he was going no place.

~~~

"Moose." Charlie said. "The kids are in bed and I think we need to talk."

Moose knew that this was coming. He had wondered how long it would take Charlie to tell him to get out. "Okay, Charlie."

"Let's go for a ride. I want to show you something."

Charlie saddled Joe and a big bay horse called, Windy. Moose watched carefully because he wanted to know how the saddle thing worked. Charlie took the horses into the yard.

"You ride, Windy, he's very gentle."

Moose looked at the saddle and wondered how it worked, how he had to get on it. Charlie looked over at him. "You don't know how to mount a saddled horse?"

"I never used one."

"Okay. Watch me."

Moose approached Windy and attempted to mount. It took him three times before he accomplished it.

Charlie grinned at him. "I knew you could do it."

They rode in silence until Charlie finally stopped. He pointed down into the valley below them.

"The Cherokee tribes settled in this area a long time ago. Down below they built and lived in villages. Over there," he pointed to the east, "they built large seven-sided buildings for their ceremonies. There are still three standing.

All of this land was their homes, they lived here and protected the land and everything it represented. They practiced long-standing traditions. Good traditions, they were and still are a spiritual people."

"You sound like you know a lot about them."

"Sam Walking Tall is a friend of mine. I learned a lot about the Cherokee nation from him."

"Why did you bring me out here?"

"To explain why you have to leave." He extended his arm and pointed, "look out there."

Moose looked at some of the most beautiful land he had ever seen, there was nothing like this in his time. "It is beautiful."

"Sometimes on a really dark night, when the wind is just right, the moon hides behind the clouds and that's when you can hear them. The Cherokee, their dead, you can hear their cries all through this valley. They sing songs that float on the wind and the drum sounds in the distant hills over there."

Charlie got down from Joe and stood silently looking into the valley. Moose also dismounted and stood next to him.

"The hills echo with the cries of the dead Cherokee as they do their war dances. Long ago, In the far distance, fires from the camps glow hot while warriors dance to the Great Spirit asking for protection in the war against the white man.

This land is a strange place, it has noises that can't be understood. The cries of the cat can sound like a woman crying in her lodge. The wolf's call is like an old man talking. If your heart is pure, it is said that the winds also will call to you, but you can't answer them, you can only listen. It's all part of the heritage and culture of the Cherokee. Sometimes, if you listen, really carefully to the wind, you can hear the Cherokee singing to the Great Spirit to save these lands that they love. All of this needs to be saved for the generations to come." Charlie turned to Moose. "I love this land that a long time ago belonged to the Cherokee. For as far as you can see this was their homelands. I feel an obligation to protect the land and somehow, I feel that you are a threat to that and that's why I have to ask you to leave."

"I assure you, Charlie, I am not was trying to destroy this land, but I am trying to stop what is going to."

Charlie was more confused than ever, but Moose wouldn't say anymore. He was actually happy when Moose told him he would be leaving in a few days. The problem was solved.

The next morning, Charlie walked into the kitchen and stood at in the doorway frowning. "Boo, what did I tell you about making coffee?"

Boo turned to her brother and smiled, "I didn't use the stove. I used the coffee maker." She said pointing to it. "Moose likes coffee."

Moose was sitting at the table and raised his cup. "Interesting and delicious."

Charlie walked over and sat down next to Boo. He sipped his coffee and frowned at her. "This coffee could raise the dead."

She lowered her eyes and asked, "too much?"

"Yes, too much. Just how many scoops of coffee did you use?"

"Boo held up a wooden spoon. "One scoop for each cup."

Charlie groaned. "That explains a lot." He picked up a teaspoon. "This is the right spoon to use. That one is too big."

Boo looked at the two spoons. "Oh, yeah, I remember now."

"Don't forget you have a piano lesson today. Miss Cornelia will be here at four. Come on, into the family room and practice."

Boo dragged herself away from the table. "Why do I have to play the piano?" She whined.

"So, you'll be well rounded." Brandon interjected.

Boo turned and glared at Brandon. "What exactly is well-rounded?"

"So, you act right in polite society." Brendan smirked.

Boo plopped down on the piano bench and looked at the keys.

"I don't think I want to be acceptable." She grumbled.

"Sure, you do." Brandon laughed. "Besides your good at the piano."

Boo groaned and put her hands on the keys. She started to play. She was not only good, she was very good, a true natural who actually enjoyed the piano even though she would never admit it. There were times when she enjoyed getting lost in her music.

Moose heard the music and followed the sound. He stood silently in the doorway and watched as Boo closed her eyes and played a beautiful melody. He couldn't believe that she played just like a professional. Charlie was right, she was an exceptional little girl.

Moose sat down on a chair and looked around at this family, this house. He thought of the ranch and all the strange animals he had seen. He thought about the land and the stories that Charlie had told him. Charlie loved the land and he considered it his responsibility to protect it. He would have to leave tomorrow, find Jackson and Chan Dana. Hopefully he could save this world for them. Right now, he leaned back and listened to Boo's music.

Chapter 12

Chan Dana was only a few steps ahead of Jackson. They were both in Atlanta. She had changed her appearance. Her long red hair was now short, and a light brown color. She couldn't do anything about her height, but she did change her four-inch heels for flat shoes. She dressed conservatively. She had stolen clothes from a store called, Watson's stop.

Chan Dana had the same problems that Jackson did, she didn't have any conventional money for this time, but she did have a plan to acquire it. It was a simple plan; she would just take it from someone.

Chan Dana had seen Jackson when she accidentally ran across him in the underground. She spotted Jackson coming out of the store and immediately ducked behind a large pillar. She followed behind him to watch where he was going. She would have to eliminate him, but there were too many people around right now and the last thing she needed was a confrontation with the local authorities. She thought that they called them, the police.

Chan Dana continued to follow behind him at a distance so that he would not see her. He would be the first, and after she had disposed of him, she would go after Morris. She wondered if Jackson could lead her to him, maybe she shouldn't be so fast to eliminate him.

Chan Dana knew that Morris was the more deadly of the two. He wouldn't hesitate to kill her. She thought she could bluff Jackson. She followed him for most of the day and watched as he disappeared through a door on the second floor. She looked around, there was nothing there, but debris. She smiled. "Later Jackson."

Just as Chan Dana was leaving the second floor she ran into Dude. She knew that she would have to play dumb. "Oh, I'm so glad I ran into someone, I think I'm lost."

"This entire end of the second floor is closed. You could get hurt up here, Lady."

"I thought the man downstairs said the jewelry store was up here. I believe it's called the Sparkle Jewel."

Chan Dana had no idea what a Sparkle Jewel was, she had seen the sign when she was sitting in a café watching Jackson.

"That store is downstairs almost directly below us. You better not come up here again, it's not safe."

"Thank you, young man."

Chan Dana walked down the stairs and never looked back. She hoped the kid wouldn't remember her. She decided to go and visit this store called, Sparkle Jewel. She waited until it started to go dark and then slipped in. There were people in their so she stunned them with the blank timer and walked out of the store with one thousand, three hundred and thirty-four dollars. She didn't bother with the coins because she had no idea what to do with them.

~~~

Moose told Boo that he had to leave. She was sitting on the steps with him, out on the porch. She pulled Connery close to her and asked, "why?"

"I can't stay here forever. I'm very grateful to you and your family for helping me, but it's time for me to move on."

"It's the man you're looking for, isn't it?"

"It's important to find him. I'll probably start in Atlanta."
~~~

"That's kind of far. Maybe Charlie can take you in the truck."

Moose wasn't sure exactly what a truck was, he knew about cars, but a truck? Maybe the truck was the same thing as a car, he had read about them and how they took you from one place to another.

"Is a truck like a car, or a horse?"

Bree looked at him and said slowly, "horses are real. They breathe. Trucks are metal, machines, like the car only bigger."

Moose move closer to Boo and leaned down. "How do trucks work?"

"You put gas in them and then start them with a key."

"Gas?"

"How do you go places where you're from?"

"With the transporters."

"I don't understand."

"The air currents do it. You program where you need to go and get on a sky lift and it takes you where you need to go."

"Does it fly like an airplane?"

"What's an airplane?"

Bree pointed up. "They fly in the sky."

"How?"

"I think you better go ask Charlie, and go with him in the truck."

"Maybe you're right."

Boo took Moose's hand in hers. "Will I ever see you again? Will you come back and see me?"

"I don't know if I can come back."

"Not ever?"

"Boo, when I go home, I may not be able to return here."

Moose couldn't tell her what horrible conditions the future was in. Could he return? He made not even get out of this time alive.

"I have a little girl, her name is Kara, she's a little younger than you are and when I go back, I'm going to tell her all about you and your wonderful ranch."

"Maybe you should come back and bring Kara with you. I would like to meet her. I could show her Connery."

Moose pulled Boo into his arms. "I'll miss you."

"When do you have to leave?"

"Probably in two days."

Boo dug into her pocket and pulled out a little blue stone she had found last year "I found this on the ridge where the Cherokee use to live. It's a real special. It will protect you."

Moose took the blue stone. He carefully placed it into his front pocket. "Thank you, Boo. Every time I look at it, I will think of you."

~~~

Chan Dana opened the newspaper and to her surprise, there on the front page was a picture of Morris Duffy. She carefully read the paragraph under the picture. He was in a town called Tustin.

She laughed wildly, "I got you." She threw down the paper. "Your dead."
~~~

Dude poured Jackson and himself a cup of coffee. Jackson wondered for the fifth time if he should be involving this boy in his search for Bill. He had spotted Chan Dana, and while she thought she was following him; he was watching her.

"Hey, Jackson." Dude said. "Did you run into the woman that was up here?"

He had been thinking about Chan Dana. She had found out where he was at. He wondered why she hadn't tried to kill him yet. Why did she just walk away?

He glanced over at Dude. "What woman?"

"A tourist, I guess, she said she got lost. Said she was looking for the Sparkle Jewel and the funny thing is they got robbed later that night."

While Dude was talking, Jackson picked up the paper he had thrown on the table. He saw the picture that she had probably seen. He threw back on the table and pointed to a picture, "Bill Trader."

"Who's Bill Trader?"

"The man I'm looking for. Do you know where Tustin, Georgia is?"

"Yeah, about 70 miles from Atlanta."

"I have to go there. I have to find him. Warn him."

Dude got up. "Warn him about what?"

"Chan Dana." Jackson went to the refrigerator and pulled it out. He couldn't leave the Sundowner here. If he couldn't make it back and it fell into someone else's hands, it would be a disaster. He opened the electrical box, picked out the Sundowner and shoved the device into his jeans pocket.

"What is that?"

"Better you don't know. We're going to need the weapons."

"You planning on fighting someone, Jackson?"

Jackson handed Dude one of the pistols. "Only if it comes to that."

Dude took the gun and placed it in his belt. "I'm with you, man." He shook his head. "I don't know why, but I am."

They stepped out of the door and a shot ring out hitting Jackson. Dude raised his pistol, pushed Jackson back inside and returned fire.

Several more shots rang out hitting the closed door. "Damn, Jackson, who the hell is that?"

Suddenly, everything went still. Chan Dana quickly retreated down the stairs and into the waves of people entering the underground.

Dude went to open the door. Cautiously, he pulled it open a crack. When he didn't see anyone, he went down the hall and over to the stairs leading to the underground. He found no one. He quickly went back to Jackson.

Jackson lay just inside of the door. Dude went down onto his knees and shook him, "Jackson."

"Still here."

"You're bleeding. We have to get your shirt off."

Dude got Jackson over to the bathroom and sat him on the toilet seat. He helped strip him out of the shirt.

"It doesn't look too bad. A lot of blood, but it's just a crease across your shoulder."

"It hurts like hell."

"I'll bet it does."

Dude cleaned the wound, and got the bleeding stopped. "I have to go and get some bandages. Will you be okay alone for a while."

"I'll be fine."

Dude made Jackson as comfortable as he could in the chair. "I'll be back in a little while."

Dude was almost down the stairs when he did a turnaround and went back to Jackson. He handed him the rifle. "Anyone tries to come in here and it's not me, shoot them."

"I will."

"I'll yell so you know that it's me."

Dude went to the nearest drugstore and bought antibiotic cream and bandages. As an afterthought he grabbed some Advil. As he was walking out, he saw a display, and grabbed a six pack of Coke.

He walked through the underground until he reached the stairs leading to the second floor, he ran up the stairs, but stopped short in front of the door. He had heard the click of a rifle.

"It's me, Jackson, don't shoot me."

"Come on in."

Dude went to work immediately. He expertly cleaned the wound, applied the antibiotic ointment and bandaged it. He had taken care of injured animals at the farm he lived on until he left so this was no big deal to him. He gave Jackson three Advil and a glass of water.

"It will help with the pain."

"I think I need to lie down for a while. Tomorrow, first thing we have to go to this town of Tustin. If Chan Dana is after me, she will also go after Bill."

Dude didn't say anything, but he knew that Jackson was going be really sore tomorrow. He helped him onto the bed.

"Hang on."

Dude went and got a Coke, went back to the bed and handed it to Jackson. "Try this. You'll love it."

Jackson looked at the bottle and smelled the brown liquid. He shrugged and took a long drink. He grinned widely. "You're right. This is great."

After Dude was sure that Jackson had been settled and as comfortable as possible, he went back to the kitchen. He pulled a chair over and sat in front of door. He laid the rifle across his lap. He was determined that no one would get past him. For the tenth time he wondered what he had gotten himself into.

Chapter 13

Chan Dana was in a town called Threadgill, it was approximately 50 miles outside of Tustin. She had arrived that evening. She walked through the town and came to a motel called, Rio's Last Stop. She wondered what the sign meant, but dismissed the thought immediately because it didn't matter. She was here to try and change history. If she could destroy both Jackson Ramon Garcia and Bill Trader, or Morris Duffy, or whatever he was calling himself these days, she could make everything right. She could save her father, Peter Ripken Ray. If she could pull it off, they could conquer the world of this time.

In this time, it would be child's play to overpower these people. Killing them would be easy. She would enjoy eliminating most of these inhabitants. The rest would be enslaved and forced to do their bidding at all times, or die. This way she could be almost sure of stopping her father's death and that was why she was here, to do anything necessary to stop his death. She would kill all that were responsible.

Chan Dana checked in the motel and paid with the money she had stolen from a man, Mr. Chester Henson. She had killed him two days before when she went to the Sparkling Jewel store in the underground. She had obtained six hundred and thirty dollars from Chester's pocket.

The young boy behind the desk said that the room would cost seventy-five dollars for the night. Chan Dana looked at the money in her hand. She didn't know which bills would make seventy-five dollars. She handed six of the bills to the young man. He looked up at her.

"That's too much." He said and handed her back two twenty-dollar bills and a five. "Room 212, the elevators down the hall to the left."

She looked at the money her hand and then put it in her pocket "thanks."

Chan Dana walked over to the elevator and stood in front of it. "Open, take me to room 212." Nothing happened.

Terry Roller, the clerk, had been watching her carefully. He walked down the hall and smiled at her. He leaned over and pressed the button. When the elevator arrived, he pointed to the button panel inside. "Hit number 2."

She got in the elevator and hit number 2. She felt the elevator jerk as it went upward. When it got to the second floor, it abruptly stopped and the doors opened. She got off the elevator and looked down the hall. There were many doors so she started to walk down and read the numbers on the rooms. When she found 212, she used the plastic key card she had been given.

Chan Dana slowly walked around the room and observed everything. She wondered what the square box on the table was for, but dismissed it. She sat on the bed and opened the travel case next to her. Inside she found what she was looking for, her Sundowner and the locator.

If Bill Trader, or Jackson switched on their Sundowners to go back, she would know. She knew that they weren't aware of this detection devices, or if they even existed. She'd gotten the device from Alvin Sandura, a brilliant researcher she had known since childhood. He came to her with his experimental prototype and made her aware of not only the possibility of time travel, but the tracking ability of the travelers. Alvin had proudly taken her into his confidence.

He had asked for a meet with her. This meeting had taken place before Chan Dana and her father destroyed 90% of Earth's population.

Chan Dana was fascinated with the whole concept of traveling through time. She spent over two months with Alvin in his private laboratory learning more. He had managed to steal a Sundowner, or borrow it for a great length as he put it, and created the tracking device.

After she learned all, she could from Alvin, she killed him. It was a bright Thursday afternoon, around 2 PM, when she showed up at Alvin Sandura's home. He answered the door and was delighted to see her again.

"It's going to be a dark day." Chan Dana said sweetly.

Alvin looked out at the sky. "It's not that dark today. Some of our days of gotten lighter. Maybe one day the sun will actually come through again."

Chan Dana smiled. She wasn't referring to the constant dim skies around them. She looked up and thought that the sky was actually a little lighter today. Alvin lived in a house in the Purple Zone of town.

All the land had been cordoned off into sections with each designating the people who lived there, Purple Zone held its intellects. Those were the people who were privileged and allowed to receive either schooling of some type, or technical innovations.

Everyone was tested at an early age, between the ages of four and six, to see if they retained specialized skills in the arts or sciences. Those that showed special understandings of various subjects would be instilled into the program. The program would further their skills and give them the opportunity to live in the Purple Zone. The Purple Zone was more advanced than the rest of the earth. It afforded more luxuries. The people deemed exceptional were placed here to live and study. Alvin was brilliant in his field.

Chan Dana sat across from Alvin in his comfortable sitting area. Surrounding them were stacks of learning devices. Since Books were rare most of his studies were on air tapes, or discs. She picked up an orange disc and regarded it. She would never understand the technical side of everything and toss it away from her.

Alvin put several glasses of Aquapura in front of her, there was a choice Aquapura, or Coquelicot. Each offered nourishment to sustain the body. She detested both, but drank the Coquelicot because she hadn't had anything to eat in days.

Chan Dana thought it was a shame she had to kill someone she knew for such a long time, but they had a secret together. She always maintained that a secret was only a secret if one person alone knew it. Alvin had to die.

Chan Dana opened her pack that was strapped to her waist, she took out a slim device that was metallic and look somewhat like a pencil. It was appropriately called, the eliminator. She pointed at Alvin.

Alvin had been looking down at his Aquapura drink, when he looked up, he saw Chan Dana pointing the weapon at him. He had just enough time to register surprise before she directed the red beam at him. Alvin glanced down at the hole in his chest and crumbled into a heap next to a small table. His body was already being consumed by the beams light. It was melting away and would soon be nothing more than a slick stain of the former person that no longer existed.

"Sorry. Bye, old friend."

Chan Dana left her memories of Alvin where they should be, in the past, and lay down on the bed. She wondered how people at this time could sleep in something this soft. It really didn't matter and she needed to sleep because tomorrow she would go to this town of Tustin and find Morris Duffy. It was time to eliminate him for good.

She had observed the cars that ran like the large ants in her time. People sat inside these things called cars; it is what she would need to travel to this town of Tustin. A young woman named Susan Freeman had given her a ride to this town. She almost killed her, but decided she was no threat and let the giggly sixteen-year-old go on her way.

Chan Dana closed her eyes and sneered, "this will be a problem for tomorrow."

~~~

The next morning, Chan Dana felt rested and her mind clear. She looked out of the motel window, it was raining. Fat drops of rain hit the window and slid down. She quickly got dressed and ready to leave. She needed to acquire a car so she could go and find Morris. She checked her eliminator and secured it in her pocket.

Briefly, she wondered if she could operate a car. "It doesn't really matter. I'll have whoever drive me over to this town of Tustin and then it's bye-bye driver."

Chan Dana took her small bag and left the room. By the time she had gotten downstairs the rain had stopped. She walked by the clerk who was behind the desk. It was not the same boy, but a young woman this time, she waved.

Once outside she looked for a likely person who would give her a ride. She would pick a teenager. She had walked until she found an outside eatery and there were several young people sitting at a large table. She went over and smiled at them.
~~~

Chan Dana was a very beautiful woman and one who knew how to manipulate people. She sat down on the bench next to the boy she had picked for her victim. She leaned against him and when he looked over at her she smiled again.

"I was wondering if you'd be available to drive me over to the town of Tustin."

"That's about 50 miles from here." The kid said, "why would I drive you over there?"

"Because I'm willing to pay, and pay well."

"How much, lady?"

"Five hundred dollars."

"All I have to do is drive you there?"

"That's it. I just need a ride."

The boy held out his hand. "You've got yourself a driver, my name is Phil Wolf."

"Meet your passenger and benefactor. Names, Laura."

Chan Dana and Phil Wolf left an hour later. Most of the road to Tustin was nothing more than a one lane highway. There was little traffic on it.

She'd been surprised when the kid led her to an old nineteen sixty-six Chevy. She looked critically at the car. "What happened to the car top?"

"It's a convertible."

"Really. Do you think you can show me how to drive this convertible?"

"Yeah. Sure. Wait until we get out of town and onto one of the back roads."

They were about 20 miles from Tustin when Phil pulled off to secondary road. "This should work." he turned to Chan Dana. "Have you ever driven a car before?"

"Actually, no."

"Great. Let's try real hard not to wreck my car."

Chan Dana sat behind the steering wheel. Phil handed her the car keys. She stared at them in her hand.

"You have to start the car." Phil said from the passenger seat.

Chan Dana looked at the dashboard. Nothing was even vaguely familiar to her. She turned to him and shrugged.

He pointed to where the keys would go. "Put the key in and turn to the right."

The car roared into life immediately. She laughed. Phil explained how everything in the car worked and soon Chan Dana was ready to try to drive.

"Go slow to start, he's down on the gas pedal."

It didn't take long before Chan Dana had mastered how to drive a car. She actually enjoyed the whole process. After she got rid of Phil, she planned on keeping the car.

Chan Dana drove to Tustin and stopped at a little restaurant called, William's Water Hole. She turned to Phil, "are you hungry?"

"You bet, and I need to stretch my legs."

She pointed to the odd shaped building before them. "Do you think we can get something to eat in there?"

"Sure, why not."

"What do you call that building?"

Phil looked at the restaurant. It was oddly shaped, looked like an old train car that someone had converted into an eatery.

He grinned, "it's a converted train car."

"Train car?"

Phil grinned, "follow me, before I starve to death."

Chan Dana stared at the menu, but she had no idea what any of these items were. She ordered the same thing that Phil did. They had a large breakfast of bacon, eggs, toast, with pancakes on the side. She watched as he started to devour his food, and then she ate hers.

Chan Dana's looked carefully at the glass orange juice in front of her. She wondered if it would taste as good as everything else, she had just eaten. Cautiously, she smelled the glass and then drank it.

After they left the Williams Water Hole they continued into Tustin. Phil drove this time.

"Where do you want to go?"

"Phil, I could use more help. I'm looking for a man, his name is Morris Duffy." Chan Dana showed him the newspaper article with Moose's picture. "If you help me find him there's an extra five hundred dollars in it for you."

Phil studied the picture carefully, he didn't know this man, but he didn't think twice and agreed to help her. It would be easy money. He would have a thousand dollars and that was more money than he had seen in a long time. All he had to do was ask around and find out where this guy lived. He would check out the local school and hangouts where the kids went. Kids had big mouths.

It didn't take long for Phil to find out the location of Morris. He went back to the motel where they had taken a room. The Reynolds Landing was your standard motel, nothing fancy, but nice and clean. Chan Dana was waiting for him.

"I got the information from some grade school kids who are friends with a kid's named Brandon. This Brandon kid lives on some kind of cattle ranch about 20 miles east of town. Seems this guy you're looking for got hurt somehow and wound up there. As far as this kid knew he still there. He said this Morris was weird."

Chan Dana went to her bag and took out a wad of bills. She didn't care how much money there was because Phil had outlived his usefulness and it was time to take care of this problem. She handed him the money.

Phil took the money out of her hand and looked at it. "This looks like more than five hundred dollars."

"You did a good job. Take the money."

Phil had never seen so much money in his life. He quickly counted it, there was over fifteen hundred dollars. He held up the money, "are you sure?"

"Absolutely."

Phil sat down on the bed and counted the money again; he was already planning what to do with it. He was going to get his girlfriend, Alice Moran, and go on a long vacation. Just the two of them. They could get away from all the bull shit in the world with this money.

He turned around to tell Chan Dana of his plan when he felt a warming sensation hit him. He was dead before he hit the floor.

Chan Dana took the car keys from his pocket and watched as his body started to disintegrate.

Chapter 14

Jackson and Dude were driving towards Tustin. It was late in the sun was beginning to set, Jackson's shoulder was aching and they knew that they would soon have to stop. He didn't want to stop because he felt Chan Dana's presence in the area. Somehow, he just knew that she was here, and not that far away.

Dude noticed Jackson grimace and asked, "are you alright?"

"Yes, and no. My shoulders really hurting me."

"There's a motel not far from here, maybe we should stop for the night."

"I need to find Bill."

"Well, it's gonna rain, we aren't going to find him tonight. You need to rest, and we don't even know where he is. Let's get a room, and first thing in the morning I'll check around and see if I can get his address."

"Chan Dana's here. I know she is. I can feel her."

"Now, who is Chan Dana?"

"She's a part of this. She'll kill Bill if she gets the chance. He has to be warned before she finds him, I need to get to him first."

Dude pulled into the Tustin Inn and got a room for them. He asked, James Tobin if he knew Bill Trader. He said he did not. Dude went back to the car and helped Jackson into the motel room and onto the bed.

"You don't look so good."

"I'll be okay."

Dude felt Jackson's forehead. "You have a fever. I'll be right back."

Dude went back to talk to the desk clerk. "My friend is running a fever. Do you have a doctor in this town?"

"We do. Dr. Dillon Bartlett. I can give him a call for you if you want."

"Yeah, maybe you better send him to our room. Can I get some Tylenol somewhere?"

"I think I might have some in the back. Hold on a minute."

James Tobin came back with a bottle of Tylenol and handed it to Dude. "What is your friend's name?"

"Why?"

"I have to tell Dr. Bartlett something."

"Jackson, his name is Jackson."

"I'll give him a call and send him over to the room."

"Thanks, man."

Dude went back to the room. Jackson was barely awake but he managed to get to Tylenol into him before he completely crashed. He covered him with a blanket and dimmed the lights. He went across the room and sat down in a large overstuffed chair and picked up the local newspaper that someone had left in the room.

An hour later there was a soft knock at the door. Dude answered it, before we found a very good-looking man, he stood 6 foot tall, or taller. He had longer brown hair with eyes that almost matched.

"I'm Dr. Bartlett. Jimmy called and said that there was a sick man?"

"Come on in. My friend Jackson, he injured his shoulder a few days ago. I'm Dude."

"Let's go have a look."

Dude shook Jackson. "Jackson, I called the doctor. You need to wake up and talk to him."

Jackson forced himself into a sitting position. He shook hands with Dillon. "Thank you for coming."

"Your friend, Dude, said you hurt your shoulder a few days ago."

"It was a construction accident." Dude lied. "We're working on my house and Jackson got hit by a bunch of wood and debris."

Jackson looked over at Dude, but said nothing.

Dillon examined Jackson's shoulder. The wound was infected, but it didn't look like a wound caused by construction accident. It looked like a crease from a bullet.

"Are you sure this was an accident?"

Jackson kept a completely straight face when he said, "yes, sir."

"You going to need antibiotics, you have a pretty good infection going there. I'll call Milt Logan and get his boy, Johnny to run over and get them for you."

Dillon re-bandaged Jackson's wound and explained to him how to take the antibiotics. Jackson thanked the doctor. He went down the hallway to the bathroom to wash his hands.

Jackson glanced over at the table next to the bed he was sitting on. Staring at him from the newspaper was Bill Trader, but they had his name wrong. He grabbed the paper and read the article under Bill's picture.

"That's him. Dude, this is Bill." He said pointing at the newspaper.

Dillon was standing in the doorway and walked over to Jackson. "Do you know Moose?"

"Whose Moose?"

"The man in the picture."

Jackson held up the picture of Bill. He turned to Dillon, "this man is Bill Trader. He is also known as Morris Duffy back in our time. He's my friend, a very good friend, and I have been looking for him for a very long time."

Dillon sat on the chair next to Jackson. "How do you know Moose, ah, Bill Trader or Morris Duffy?"

"Why do you call him Moose?"

Dillon smiled "a little girl named Boo asked him his name and she thought he said Moose. He actually said Morris, but Moose stuck."

"Well, his real name is Bill Trader. I have known him since we were children. We went to school together and then we work together. Our lives have always been interconnected, but he got lost to me, and I need to find him."

"What kind of work did you do together?"

Jackson thought about everything he had learned about this time. "We were in law enforcement together."

"Moose, Bill, let's just stick to Moose, it's a lot easier, was injured when we found him. Charlie found him on his property down by the river about six weeks ago. He had a head wound and afraid he doesn't remember much about his past."

"Exactly how bad is Bill hurt?"

"He has recovered with the except of his memory, he's doing well. He plans on leaving in a few days, but I don't think he really knows where he is going to go."

"He'll be going home, with me."

"You're going to need a little time to heal yourself. You've got a fever and an infection."

"There was a knock on the door. Johnny smiled at Dillon. "Got your prescription, Doc. Anything else I can do for you?"

"You've done enough. Thank your father for opening the pharmacy."

"Sure, Doc. Later."

Dude looked over at Dillon and asked, "it's Sunday, how did you make that work?"

"Small town, everybody knows everyone else and we all kind of cooperate with each other."

After Johnny left, Dillon gave Jackson one of the antibiotics and explained how he should take them.

"Thank you, sir."

"Before I leave, why don't you tell me how you got the gunshot wound."

In that instance, Jackson decided to tell the doctor the truth. Who he was, who Bill Trader was, and more importantly why he was here. He hoped it wasn't a mistake.

"There's a woman name, Chan Dana Ray, she's a very sought-after criminal, very dangerous, lethal, and she wants both Bill and myself dead. She did this to me. The man that you call Moose has been tracking her for a long time. If his memory is as bad as you say he won't know that she is after him. I have to warn him."

Jackson stopped, he wanted to see what the doctor's reaction would be before he said anymore. He watched him very carefully.

Dillon didn't know what to say. Moose has been a mystery since the day he met him, and now this man, Jackson was just as puzzling. "I don't understand what's going on here."

"I'm not sure you would believe me if I told you the truth, and I would really understand if you didn't."

"Try me."

Jackson took a deep breath and sighed; he would give him the short version of what was going on. When he told him that Bill Trader and he were from the Earth's future, he could see the doubt in his eyes. Dude listened carefully but didn't react to anything that Jackson had just said.

"I know it's a lot to understand, and I also understand if you don't want to believe it, but all of its true. We're the law 500 hundred years plus from now where Chan Dana is very dangerous, she is wanted on the earth and out stations of the globe. You have to understand that she could destroy this time."

"If that's true, it explains a lot about Moose. If everything you're telling me is the exact truth, I understand why Moose didn't know what a stove was, or how to use it. He didn't even know what a Connery was."

"Who's Connery?"

"Connery, is a dog."

"There aren't many dogs in the future, and the ones left are not allowed in the public. They're trying to preserve the species."

"No dogs?"

"Our lives are very different in the future. There are very few animals left in our world. We only know of this time by going to what is equivalent to one of your museums. We have several places that tell us of the past. I understand Bill's confusion because there are many things here that I don't recognize or know of either. I need your help, Doctor, I'm trying to save not only your world, but our future."

Chapter 15

Chan Dana left the car out of sight and slowly worked her way down to the ranch house. The sky was turning dark so she had the advantage of not being seen easily. She stayed hidden behind the bushes close to the house.

She spotted Moose near the barn with a child. They had an animal with them that she didn't recognize. Moose was sitting close to the animal and leaning into it.

"Moose," Boo laughed. "That's not how you milk a cow."

Moose looked up at the cow and said, "she's just not cooperating, or maybe she's empty."

"She is cooperating, and she has milk, all she has to do is stand there, you're the one that has to do the work. Here, let me show you again."

Boo expertly got the milk flowing. "See, you have to squeeze gently and pull slowly."

"Okay. Let me try again. Are you sure she won't bite me?"

"She won't. She never bites."

"How about kicking?"

"She won't kick you either."

Boo patted the cow. "Be patient with Moose, he's new at this." She explained to her.

Chan Dana pointed her eliminator at Moose and yelled, "Morris Duffy."

Moose jumped up kicking the bucket that held the milk. He turned to face Chan Dana. The first thing he saw was the device eliminator device that she held in her hand.

"Who is that?" Boo whispered.

Moose pushed Boo behind him and said, "Boo, go into to the barn, right now."

Boo looked over at Chan Dana. She instantly didn't like her and was instantly afraid of her.

"Boo, go."

"The kid stays." Chan Dana yelled.

Boo grabbed Moose's arm. This woman was scaring her.

"Let the kid go, she's no part of this."

"No, I have a feeling you'll behave better if we keep her here. Before I take care of you, I need to know where Tanocka Burns is."

"What makes you think I know where he is?"

"He was following you."

"Sorry to disappoint you Chan Dana, but I have no clue where Tanocka Burns is at. Why do you even want him?"

"I guess there's no harm in telling you because I'm going to kill you so you can't tell anyone else. I need him to stop my father's death."

"Let Boo go. She's just a little kid and doesn't understand any of this."

Chan Dana looked carefully at the little girl for the first time. Maybe she could use her to her advantage.

"I will hurt the kid. All you have to do is tell me where Tanocka Burns can be found."

Moose was slowly moving towards Chan Dana. He needed to get close enough to disarm her, if that was going to be possible. He also wanted Boo out of harm's way.

"Stop! Don't come any closer."

Chan Dana aimed the eliminator directly at Moose. Boo realized that this was some type of weapon and screamed. She ran forward and pushed at Chan Dana almost knocking her over.

"You leave my Moose alone." She yelled.

Moose bolted forward, but Chan Dana was quick to recover and grabbed Boo while she shot at him. He felt something push at his chest and collapsed.

Chan Dana dragged Boo behind her. She was furious that Chan Dana had hurt Moose. "You let go of me. I have to help my Moose."

"You can't help him, he's dead."

Boo screamed at her. "You killed my Moose." She started to cry. "Let me go. I hate you."

"Shut up, or I'll kill you too."

She was almost to the car with Boo when she stopped. A big black-and-white animal was blocking her path. She wasn't sure what it was, but its lips were curled back and she saw its teeth.

Connery stood his ground. He growled and admitted a low menacing warning. Chan Dana pointed the eliminator at him. Boo quickly grabbed her arm.

"No. I'll make him go home."

Boo went over to Connery and wrapped her arms around him. "Stop. It's alright. You go home, Connery. Go home to Brandon. Go on now. Hurry."

Connery took two steps forward and stopped. "Go home, Connery. Go home."

Connery moved slowly toward the barn looking back every few steps. When he got to the barn, he found Moose and lay down next to him.

Chan Dana grabbed Boo by the arm and pushed her into the backseat of the car. Boo was scared, her thoughts went back to Moose and she started to cry.

"Shut up, kid."

Tears slipped down her cheeks and her voice wavered as she said, "you killed my Moose."

"He had to go. Now, I got a fine Tanocka Burns myself. I know he's here. It makes sense that he would come here. I have to find him."

"Who is he?"

"He's the man I have to kill to save my father, and you, are going to help me make that happen."

"I can't kill anyone."

"You're my insurance."

Boo didn't understand what she was talking about and she was so scared she was afraid to move. She didn't know who this woman was, but she was definitely scary. How could she help her? What did being her insurance mean? Why would she even think that she would help her? She needed to go home. Charlie would be worried. And Moose? She decided she couldn't think about Moose right now because that would make her cry. She wondered where this woman was taking her.

"This will bring Jackson straight to me. Once he's gone, I can kill Tanocka Burns without any interference."

"Who's Jackson?"

"Jackson is the man who is hunting me. I'm going to let him find me. He'll follow because of you, and then I will have the total advantage."

Chan Dana didn't care if Boo knew her plans because she had no intentions of letting her go. Once Jackson was dealt with, she would have no further use for her. She would probably have to kill her.

She assumed that Morris was already working with Jackson. Morris tried to protect this child which meant Jackson would also want to protect her. He would come after her and right into her waiting hands.

"I don't know who Jackson is."

"I'm sure you do."

"I want to go home."

"I can't let that happen."

Chan Dana turned the car into the motel lot where she was staying. She parked in front of her room and then turned to Boo.

"Get out. Follow me and don't give me any trouble or you will regret it. Move! Now!"

Boo got out of the back of the car and was grabbed by the arm. Chan Dana had changed motels and was now at one called, Starlight Inn, it was off of Highway #16. She liked it because it was tucked away in the hillside. She had purposely asked for the first-floor room. It was nothing more than a small strip motel with about twenty-five rooms. She had picked one in the back that faced a freeway above it. It was perfect because no one would bother her here, or ask any questions. She had the highway on one side protecting her and the mountains on the other.

Chan Dana hadn't been prepared for taking Boo with her. She wasn't sure what to do with her. Usually, she just killed her victims outright, but in her mind, she needed this kid to get to Jackson.

She opened the door and shoved Boo into the room.

"Go sit in the chair over there and don't move."

Boo slowly walked away from her, backing up until she hit the table. She sat down in the chair, this woman scared her, but she was also getting mad. She didn't like being pushed around, but she knew she had to be careful because this evil woman had killed her Moose. Tears welled up in her eyes but she fought them. She knew that she got the opportunity she would have to try to get away. Even at the young age of nine she knew that this woman would kill her without thinking twice about it.

Boo jumped up, "you just wait till Sheriff Andy Towlend finds out you stole me. He'll come here and arrest you. I hope he put you in jail for a hundred years."

"Shut up. No Sheriff is going to find me, or even arrest me. What the hell is a Sheriff?"

"He's the law, lady. He puts bad people like you would jail. You killed my Moose."

"Enough. You just sit down there and be quiet."

"I have to go to the bathroom."

Chan Dana turned to her, "what?"

"The bathroom. I got to go bad."

Chan Dana was examining the eliminator. It hadn't glowed red when she shot Morris with it, and now it was even weaker in color, almost a pale orange.

"Lady, I really need to go."

"Go. It's over there. Make it fast."

Boo got up and went into the bathroom. She closed the door and quickly looked around to see if she could escape from there. There was only one window over the bathtub area. She stood in the bath tub, but it was so high she couldn't reach it and there was nothing to stand on.

Who decided to go through everything in the bathroom, but found there was nothing to help her. She flushed the toilet and ran the water. She was wiping her hands when Chan Dana burst in.

"You've had enough time in here."

"Okay already, I'm coming."

Chan Dana went back to the table; she had taken the eliminator apart in an attempt to find out why it didn't want to work. Boo sat down across from her and watched. She wondered what she was doing.

"What is that?"

"An eliminator."

"I don't think I know what that is. What is it supposed to do, what is an eliminator?"

"It kills people."

Boo didn't ask any more about the eliminator. She had seen Chan Dana use it on Moose. Now, she knew for sure that Moose was dead. She looked at this woman, she hated her and was even more determined to get away from her as fast as she could. She needed to get the sheriff so that he could take her off to jail. She needed to go to jail.

"I'm hungry."

"What?"

"I'm hungry. I haven't eaten since breakfast it's almost dark. We need to get something to eat."

Chan Dana looked at Boo like she had two heads. She knew that she would have to feed her, but what does a kid eat, and where do you get it?"

"What do you eat?"

Both thought for a moment and then said, "food."

"What food?"

"How about cheeseburgers. Duncan Denny's shouldn't be that far from here."

"What is a Duncan Denny?"

Boo looked at her and realized she was like Moose; she didn't know much about anything. She decided that she must be from his future. Everything that he had told her was true, and this was the woman he had been searching for.

"It's a place where you go for food. They make it for you, you pay for it, and then you eat it."

"I cannot let you sit in a place where people are."

"Fine. We can get take out."

"What exactly is takeout?"

"Let's go to Duncan Denny's and I'll show you."

"No. You're not going anywhere. Explain it."

Boo took a deep breath. "You go to the restaurant," she said very slowly and patiently, as if she was speaking to someone who didn't understand anything, "order the food, pay for it, and then tell him it's to go. They put it in a bag and you take it back here."

"I'll go, you're staying here. Tell me where this place is at."

Boo thought this may be her opportunity to get away, so she gave her the directions to Duncan Danny's. She wasn't really sure that they were right because she had only been there once, she didn't care, and Chan Dana would just have to figure that one out without her help.

"You'd better let me write down what you're supposed to get."

Boo looked around and found paper and pen. She went to the table and printed out a list.

"Here, just read it to him." She smirked. "If you can't read, just hand it to him."

"You are a brat, aren't you?"

Boo didn't answer Chan Dana. She just stood next to the table and stared at her like she was crazy.

"I didn't need you; I wouldn't bother feeding you."

Chan Dana made sure that Boo was securely tied. She also put duct tape over her mouth so she couldn't yell out. At the last minute she went back and tied her to the bed.

Boo screamed at her from behind the tape.

Chan Dana left to find Duncan Danny's. She didn't realize how hungry she was.

Chapter 16

Dillon drove Jackson and Dude out to the Crawford ranch. He thought about everything that Jackson had told him. It seemed impossible to him, but also probable. Could he believe that Moose, and this man called Jackson came from the future, his future? He was inclined to not believe it. A man traveling from the future, it just wasn't logical, but stranger things had happened, things that he didn't understand, but accepted as true.

The Sky Quakes that emitted loud Booming sounds that came from the sky for no reason. The explosive rumbling came from the distance and could be heard around the world. It was strange, but true.

People who lived in Portland, Oregon, were bothered by a mysterious noise also. It sounded like a high-pitched train whistle. The sound seemed to come from nowhere and its source has never been found. It happened with a constant frequency.

There is a bubblegum pink lake in Western Australia. It's a small Salt Lake that turns from blue violet to pink. Something that's never been explained, but is true.

In the Antarctica there is a blood red waterfall that comes from ice. It flows from the McMurdo Dry Valley. This is considered one of the most inhospitable places on the earth. It's also extremely cold and the falls stand about five stories tall.

There is a type of beach where stones eerily move on their own, is called the Sailing Stones of Death Valley. Death Valley National Park is known for being the hottest, driest, place on the earth.

Rocks drift across the flat desert landscapes. They seem to be propelled under no power except their own. Because there is a gravitational pull the stones have become known as the "Sailing Stones." The strangest part is that the rocks can weigh hundreds of pounds, or just a few ounces. They leave behind them large trails. It is clear that the stones change their locations.

These were all proven facts, things that Dillon didn't understand, but there were proven true. All of this made him decide to take Jackson story with a little faith until proven differently.

When Dillon drove up to the barn, he saw someone lying by it. Connery was lying next to him. He stopped the car and went directly over to Moose.

Dillon went down to his knees. "Moose, can you hear me?"

"Yeah, am I dead?"

"No, not hardly. You think you can get up if I help you? I'll take you into the house."

"Let me help you." Dude offered and took Moose's arm.

"My head is killing me."

"Take it easy until I get you into the house."

Dillon had Moose lay down on the bed. Jackson, who had been in the background, now stood inside the door and watched the doctor carefully.

"Do you remember what happened?" Dillon asked.

Chan Dana happened. She shot me with the eliminator. Damn thing must the malfunction because I'm still here. It should have killed me."

Moose jumped up. "Boo. Doc, she took Boo."

"Who took Boo?"

"Chan Dana. I have to find her."

"What's a Boo?" Dude asked.

"Bill." Jackson said and stepped forward. He held up his hands. "Relax, I'm here after Chan Dana too. All the charges against me have been dismissed, I'll explain it all later to you. I'm here to help you. Now, who's Boo?"

"A little girl." Dillon yelled. "Where the hell did this Chan Dana take her, and why?"

"Chan Dana thought she killed me, and if she knew about Jackson, she'll be after him next. She wouldn't have taken Boo unless she thought she could use her."

"She thinks were working together. She knows we were working together. Knowing that your dead, she figures I'll follow her to get Boo back, and she's right."

"I'm going with you."

"Are you sure you're okay to do this, Bill?"

"They took Boo. She's very special and I am going to get her back."

Jackson saw a picture on the dresser and picked it up. "Who is this a picture of?"

Dillon took the picture from Jackson. "That's Boo."

"Bill, she looks just like…………"

"I know. We have to get her back, Jackson."

"But how can that be?"

"What are you two talking about?" Dillon asked. "We need to go after Boo."

Moose ignored Dillon. "We need to hurry. Jackson, I'm trusting you that you're telling me the truth."

"I am. We need to stop Chan Dana before she destroys this world."

"She has that kind of power?" Dude asked.

"She does." Moose looked at this young man standing quietly next to Jackson. "Who exactly are you?"

"He's with me." Jackson said.

"Where is everyone?"

"Who's that?" Jackson asked raising his weapon.

"Charlie." Moose said. "It's okay, Jackson, put away your gun. We don't want to shoot one of the good guys."

Jackson put his pistol back into his belt just as Charlie walked into the room. He looked at everyone and there and turned to Dillon. "What's happened here?"

They quickly explained to Charlie everything that had happened.

"We go together."

Moose examined the pistol Jackson had given him again. He turned to Charlie, "you can't come. This is for Jackson and me to do. You are no match for Chan Dana. We are going to be lucky if we make it out of this alive. I will tell you one thing, Charlie, and it's something you need to believe. I guarantee you that I will find Boo and I will bring her home to you."

He walked over to Charlie and put his hand on his shoulder. "I promise you; I will find her. You cannot come because you will only slow us down."

"I'm going with you too."

"You're staying here, Dude. I'll be back for you later."

"I want to go. I want to help you."

"You have already helped me and I appreciate it, but it's time for me to go with Bill. We've always been good together, and this is dangerous, but we've done this before."

"Jackson," Moose said. "Chan Dana is looking for Tanocka Burns. She thinks that he is here somewhere in this time, and if that's true we need to find him before she does."

"Why Tanocka Burns?"

"I'm not sure, but I think it has something to do with her stopping him so that she can save her father. She wasn't making much sense, but then I was pretty stunned by the eliminator."

"I wonder why it didn't work?" Jackson said absently as he again checked his gun. "Oh, sorry Bill, I'm really glad it didn't work or you wouldn't be here."

"Maybe she didn't realize that you have to recharge it, or maybe she didn't bring the recharging mechanism. Jackson, she has a car, and she can drive it."

Jackson looked over at Moose, "do you know how to drive one of those things?"

"Nope. I don't have a clue how it works."

Jackson turned to Dude. "You're coming after all, you're driving."

Dude looked over at Moose in Jackson, shrugged, and asked, "which way? How do we find this Chan Dana?

"Start driving south. I saw her pull out in that direction."

Moose turned to Jackson, "did you bring a tracker dog?"

"Yeah, where's yours?"

Moose shrugged. "It got busted in the transport."

"Good thing I carry a spare."

Jackson held up a small device that glowed a purplish color. All children in the future wore tracker dogs. They were inserted behind the babies left ear. It had become a necessity because of the violence in the future. A victim could immediately be found by a special team designated as the Seekers. They were an important part of the League of Law Enforcement. Many lives had been saved because of this team.

When Chan Dana and her father, Peter Rippen Ray rained their destruction on the earth, it was before members of the Seeker team were killed. Annie Wegner, Sarah Keller, Mark Vaughn, and Damien Sundance died in the first wave of destruction. The devices that they called the tracker dogs were secured by Jackson before he transported to the past. There were few that remained intact. He had taken one of them with him as a precaution.

Jackson held up the device that changed from a purplish glow to a bright turquoise. It let out a sharp bark.

"What is that?" Jackson asked.

Moose grinned at him, "it was called the tracker dog, and since I would never see a real dog, I went to the house of records and found the bark. It's just a virtual message of a dog bark."

"Okay. Fine. Works for me. Did you name it?"

"I never thought about naming it."

Dude was listening to the two men and their banter back and forth. He found a very interesting and continue to drive.

"I think we should call the tracker dog, Connery. That's Boo's dog's name."

Jackson sighed, "that was the first time I ever saw a real dog. He was very warm."

Dude shook his head, these two were really strange. *What the hell did I get into? He hoped he didn't get himself killed.*

The seeker directed them north towards Atlanta. While Moose and Jackson were using it to find Chan Dana, she was at Duncan Danny's. She looked at the note for the third time. She couldn't read Boo's writing.

She looked up at the board above the kid behind the register. She didn't know what the strange foods listed there were. The kid was right, all she knew for sure was that it was food. She finally handed the kid behind the counter the note. He looked at it and grinned.

"No problem. Be up in a minute."

"I need to take that with me."

"No problem. I'll pack it to go."

Twenty minutes later, Chan Dana was walking out with two bags and a holder with some kind of drinks and it. They were brown. She put all of it in the car. The aroma from the food was great in her stomach growled.

Chapter 17

Boo waited a few minutes to make sure that Chan Dana wouldn't come back before she started to wiggle the rope that held her. She turned and turned in an attempt to loosen the ropes. Nothing happened. She pulled her hand away from the rope and felt it give just a little. It wasn't enough.

Boo remembered a TV show she watched where the bad guy was going to tie up the good guy. The good guy, while he was being tied up, he made his hands into fists, she had done the same thing. Now, when she opened her hand, it made the rope a little bit looser. She struggled to free her hand and felt the rope slipped just a little, but it still wasn't enough.

Boo's arms ache not only from being tied up, but from her attempts to get loose. She stopped for a minute and listen for Chan Dana to see if she was coming back. Everything was quiet.

Boo continued to work the ropes for what seemed like forever. She stopped immediately when she heard someone at the door. Chan Dana walked in with both bags of food. She placed everything on the table before going over to Boo. She took out a knife and held it up to her face. Boo moved back as far as she could on the bed.

"Relax, kid, I'm just going to cut the ropes."

Boo scrambled across the bed and over to the table. She realized that she was about ready to starve. She looked into the bag and grabbed a cheeseburger and fries. She also took a chocolate shake. She glanced up at Chan Dana and then began to eat.

Chan Dana took the other bag and sat opposite her. She tried a French fry and was surprised at how good it tasted. She held one up. "What is this called?"

"It's called a French fry. Haven't you ever had a French fry before?"

"We don't have food like this where I come from."

"Bummer."

After they finish their cheeseburgers and fries, Chan Dana told Boo she was going to tie her up so she could get some sleep.

"Again?"

"Yes, again."

"I need to go the bathroom first."

"Hurry it up."

~ ~ ~

Moose looked at the tracker dog again. "How did the Seekers keep straight who they were tracking? I'm getting a lot of mixed signals here."

They were sitting in the car on route 76. They had been following Chan Dana for hours. Moose felt they were close, but then the tracker dog stopped working. It seemed to switched over to a different person."

"Let me have a look at it." Jackson said and took the device.

While Jackson was studying the tracker dog, Moose was studying him. In his heart he knew that Jackson never did all of the things he was accused of. He knew the man; he was incapable of that kind of murder.

They had known each other since they were young boys and he knew Jackson Ramon Garcia was an honest man. He didn't know why he had been so blind to that until now. They had worked together, and he had always trusted him with his life, something that happened on more one occasion.

"Jackson, what happened? Why were they after you?"

"I was cleared of all charges." Jackson stopped what he was doing. He slowly shook his head. "Chan Dana. She and that father of hers. She left me for dead, and tried to place all of the blame for what they did on me. She is so dangerous and lethal. Don't ever forget that, and don't turn your back on her."

"I never really believe that you could've done something like that."

"Then why were you hunting me for over a year?"

"For several reasons, One, they assigned me. Two, I wanted to find you before someone else did so you wouldn't get hurt, or worse killed. Jackson, I didn't find out you were declared innocent until you just told me."

Jackson grinned. "I'm glad you do believe me."

"Why wouldn't I?"

Dude was sleeping in the back seat, he yawned and said, "I'm hungry."

"We have to keep going. I have to find Boo."

"It's late. We can't do anymore tonight. Bill, even Chan Dana has to sleep sometimes."

"The minute she thinks she doesn't need Boo; she will kill her. I can't let that happen."

"It's going to take me a little while to fix this tracker dog. I need somewhere to work on it," Jackson pointed to the darkening sky. "Somewhere with light."

"There's a motel sign up the road." Dude said.

Moose felt a cloud of dark gloom hit him. He didn't want to stop, he had to continue, he had to find Boo. He couldn't let anything happen to her; he couldn't let Chan Dana happened to her.

Jackson stared at his old friend; he could almost read his thoughts. "We'll find her, Bill. How are you feeling?"

"Like I was hit with a ton of bricks."

Dude dug into his pocket and pulled out a bottle of Advil. He walked over and handed to Moose. "This might help some."

Moose held the bottle in his hands and studied it. "What is it?"

"It's like a painkiller. Take two or three and it'll work a lot faster."

Jackson shrugged. "That would work for me."

Moose downed the pills with a bottle of water. "I guess we better get to that motel."

They checked into the Creek Peach Motel. Once they got into the room Jackson suggested that Moose should lay down. He looked longingly at the bed, but went over to sit at the table.

"Let's see if we can get this tracker working."

Jackson studied his friend. His shoulder hurt like hell, so he knew that Bill was also feeling bad. Bill was sitting on the edge of the bed, "do you think you can fix it?"

"I think I can do it. I've had some experience with them. You need to lay down before you fall down."

"All I need is about an hour and then I'll be ready to go again."

Moose collapsed on the bed and was asleep instantly. Dude got up, went to the closet and pulled out a blanket to cover him. He walked over to the table and sat down next to Jackson.

"How did you and Bill get involved in all of this?"

Jackson grinned. "We are in what this time calls, Law Enforcement. Hell, we were young in our 20s when we joined the ATACA league. We were pretty wild back at that time, but it was a different time, a wild time in its own. The evil movement that now exists was just going into play."

Jackson stopped what he was doing and shook his head. "The woman was searching for, Chan Dana Ray, I knew her as Landa Masta. She's beautiful, as beautiful as she is deadly. It was easy to love her."

"How could you love her? I thought she was a ruthless killer?"

"She is all of that, but that side of her didn't emerge until later. Seemed like a switch that was pulled and the sweet, smart, extraordinarily intelligent woman turned from all of that into what she is today. She's dangerous and she wouldn't hesitate to kill. You, me, Bill, it wouldn't matter. Dude, you should walk away before you get hurt."

"I can't walk away from you and Bill, Jackson. I've been taking care of myself for a long time, and I'm not afraid. I'm not even afraid to die."

"Dude"

"Nope, I'm sticking." He grinned wildly. "Besides neither one of you can drive a car."

~~~

"I don't care what Moose says. I'm calling Andy Towlend." Charlie said as he picked up the phone.

"Do you think that Boo's all right?" Brandon asked as he absently scratched Connery's head.

Charlie looked at his little brother and saw the worry in his face. He was worried enough for both of them. "You know Boo you should worry about the person that took her."

Sheriff Towlend walked into the Crawford's home, there were several deputies with him. Kevin Waters, Mike Evers, and Tommy Ryan.

"Get started boys. The deputies immediately started to examine the area outside. Charlie went with them.

"Do you know which way they went, Charlie? Did they say anything?" Deputy Tommy Ryan wanted to know.

"No. Nothing."
~~~

Chapter 18

Boo squinted in the darkness. She didn't know that a motel room could be so dark, the only light was the little that showed through the side of the curtain on the window, but the room was still pretty dark.

She held her breath as she looked over at the other bed. She could hear the soft breathing coming from the bed. Cruella was asleep.

She had started calling Chan Dana, Cruella almost from the first moment they had met. The first time she did it, the woman looked confused, but she didn't comment on it. The second time she snapped.

"What is a Cruella?

"That's your name."

"My name is Chan Dana Ray."

"Okay, Cruella, whatever you say."

Boo giggled to herself. This was the worst villain she could think of and if it irritated her that was just too bad.

"Stop it."

"Stop what?" She said innocently.

"Look, the only reason I'm keeping you alive is because Jackson will follow you."

"I told you; I don't know who Jackson is."

"He's Bill's friend, and that means he'll try to find you and finish what Bill started, he'll be coming after you."

"Who's Bill

"What are you, dumb or something. He's your friend, the one I killed back at the ranch."

"Bill? You mean my Moose?" A tear fell from Boo's eye. She could feel her anger rise, "you're hateful, Cruella, you killed my Moose, and if Jackson comes, I hope he does the same to you."

Boo snaped back from her thoughts and looked closely at the rope that bound her hands. The rope was tight, probably too tight for her to get it loose. She had tried pulling at it and when that didn't work, she used her teeth. She needed a knife, but she was tied to the bed and there probably wasn't one in this motel room anyhow.

Boo pulled at her ropes in frustration and jerked at the bed. She heard a large crack and went still. Quickly, she looked over at Cruella and froze.

Chan Dana turned over in the bed and was now facing away from her.

Boo was almost too frightened to even move. She waited until she heard the soft snoring coming from the other bed.

Boo twisted around until she was facing the headboard. Cruella had tied her hands and attach the rope to the headboard. She studied the headboard carefully. It was wooden and the design was made up of open circles. She stood up on the bed so she was facing the circles on the headboard. She ran her hand over them. She touched something sharp. The rope that was tied to the circle on the headboard was cracked. She touched the crack lately and felt the partial break. It extended around half of the circle. She pushed against it and felt it give just a little. She smiled, maybe she could get away after all.

Boo worked on the circle rubbing the rope back and forth. She glanced at Cruella constantly to make sure that she wasn't waking up. After a while she got tired and decided she had to stop and rest for a while. She slid down onto the pillows into a seated position. She thought she would just rest for a few minutes and then try again.

Boo was startled awake when Chan Dana shook her. She had startled her and she screamed. Chan Dana slapped her.

"Stop screaming."

Boo was furious, no one had ever slapped her before. She yanked on the ropes.

"Let me go. These ropes hurt, and I gotta go to the bathroom."

Chan Dana took the knife and sliced the rope. Boo scurried off of the bed and went into the bathroom. She slammed the door behind her. She looked in the mirror. She felt as awful as she looked, her face burned where Cruella had hit her. Her head hurt, and there were red marks on her wrist where she had been tied. She felt dirty.

Boo opened the shower curtain in the tub area. There were little bottles of shampoo and body wash. She grinned and started the water. When the tub was filled, she stripped off her clothes and slipped in. She had made bubbles with the body wash and let them surround her. She almost sighed with the pleasure of it because it was the first time she felt better since she had gotten stolen from her home.

She looked at the door and sneered, "you'll be sorry for stealing me Cruella. You just wait until Dillon and Charlie find you. They'll fix you good."

There was a pound on the door. "You've been in there long enough. Let's get going."

"I can't."

"What? Why?"

"I'm taking a bath."

"A bath!!"

Chan Dana opened the door. All could she could see was Boo's head because the rest of her was submerged under the water.

"What are you doing?"

"Taking a bath. I felt dirty, and since you stole me, I don't have any clean clothes. I have to put these dirty ones back on and that's icky."

Chan Dana couldn't believe what she was hearing. She didn't understand what this child was thinking. They were on the run and there was no time for things like a bath.

This kid was a pain and she was so tempted to kill her and be done with it, but if Jackson found the body that would be a problem.

"Get moving. I don't care if you feel your clothes are dirty. Put them on, were leaving in ten minutes."

"Okay, Cruella. Don't get in a snit."

Boo wasn't as frightened of Chan Dana as she was before because she had said she needed her so someone named Jackson would come. If he did, she would try to warn him about her.

When Boo came out of the bathroom, she smiled at Cruella. "At least the inside of me is clean. I can't leave yet."

"Shut up and get ready."

"I can't."

Chan Dana stood over Boo with her hands on her hips. "Why?"

"I may need the bathroom."

"You are just in there."

"Yeah, I know, but I have to urinate a lot."

"Urinate?"

"Dillon, he's my friend, and he's a doctor, he said you shouldn't say Pee because the proper word is urinated."

"What does that have to do with anything?"

"It's a medical condition. Dillon said it's hereditary. Probably on my momma's side. I mean I never really knew her, but………."

"Stop! Get yourself moving, and keep your mouth shut for a while. One more wrong move out of you and I'll break your little neck."

"Boy, are you touchy."

Chapter 19

Charlie paced as he listened to Sheriff Towlend. He couldn't believe what was happening. Couldn't believe that they hadn't found Boo yet.

"We will keep looking. I've alerted every police station around us. We're going statewide with this. We'll find her, Charlie".

Charlie went directly up to the Sheriff, he stood staring at him for a few minutes before he said, "and what if they're no longer in the state. My little nine-year-old sister has been kidnapped by some psycho bitch. Andy, she could be dead by now. Have you thought about that?"

"You can't think that way, Charlie." Dillon said. "It won't do anyone any good."

Charlie turned to Dillon when, his voice broke when he asked, "do you think she still alive, Dillon? I don't. I did at first, but now I don't. I don't know why that woman took her. Why would she want a little girl, but I do believe she'd kill her. You know Boo, she could try the patience of a Saint. If she's too much trouble, talks too much, or just becomes a burden...........'"

Charlie didn't finish his thought. He just couldn't. He just had to stop thinking that Boo was gone forever. He walked over and collapsed into the kitchen chair.

Brandon, who had been standing in the doorway listening to his brother went over and put his arms around him. "I don't believe that Boo's dead. You know her, she's real resourceful. She might give her back just because Boo drives her crazy."

"She's only nine years old."

"Yeah, but she doesn't think like a nine-year-old."

~~~

Moose woke abruptly. The room was still dark, he laid quietly and listen, but didn't hear anything. The only thing he did hear was in the distance, it was the roar of cars from the freeway. He sat up in the bed and groaned.

"Bill?"

"Yeah."

"It still dark. Go back to sleep."

"I can't. Boo won't let me."

"I think I know why she bothers you so. She looks like Kara. In fact, she looks so much like your daughter that she could pass for her."

"I know. When I woke up and saw her for the first time it was a shock. I thought for a moment that it was Kara. Then she started to talk to me and the voice was different. Jackson, she is one sweet, kindhearted, loving little girl and I can't let Chan Dana hurt her."

"We'll find her."

"We have to, and it has to be soon."

"Let's wake up Dude and get going. She's after me, and I sure don't want to disappoint her."

"What about Tanocka Burns? Do you think she can save Peter Rippen Ray by killing him? She claimed that he was a direct link to her father's death, so, in her mind, yes, she will be after him and she will not hesitate to kill him. My worry is for Johnny Donya because if he gets in the way she won't hesitate to kill him also. He's a good agent, and a good friend. He could be in the line of fire."
~~~

"Well then, I guess we'll just have to find her first."

~ ~ ~

Boo looked at the car. "I don't think it's gonna go much further."

"Get in."

Boo put her hand on the door and repeated her statement. Chan Dana turned on her and sneered at her, "now, what are you talking about? How do you know it won't go much farther?"

"You have to put gas in it or it won't run anymore. You drove for days. Cut it on now show you what I'm talking about."

"What on?"

"The car."

Chane Dana grabbed Boo and shoved her into the passenger seat. She went around to the other side and slipped into the driver's seat and started the car.

Boo pointed to the gas gauge. "You're about empty." When Chan Dana looked confused, she pointed. "Look at the arrow, it's almost on empty. Car can't without gas."

Chan Dana had no idea where to find this gas thing, she didn't even know what it looked like. Maybe it wasn't so bad having to haul this kid around because at least she was being useful.

"Where do we go for this gas?"

"To a gas station."

Chan Dana lowered her head to the steering wheel and gritted her teeth. "Where is that?"

"I don't know. I'm not from around here and I don't believe I've ever been here before." Boo pointed to the grocery store across from the motel. "I could go in there and asked them."

"Fine. Move it. You go in and find out."

"I will, but you need to get us something to eat. Just go down the aisles and find something. I better be the one to talk to the clerk."

"I'll be watching you."

"Fine."

When they got into the small store, Boo stopped. She turned to Cruella and said, "have to go to the bathroom."

Chan Dana's eyes grew wide. "Again?"

"I told you. It's hereditary, not my fault. I don't want to wet my pants, I'm dirty enough."

Boo went to the clerk and asked for the bathroom key. Chan Dana went with her and make sure there was no way she could escape.

"Hurry it up." She sneered at her.

"Yeah. Yeah."

Boo went in and locked the door behind her. She looked around quickly. It was one room with a toilet and a sink. In the corner she spotted an old coin telephone. She saw one once in a movie, a very old movie. The man put money into it and talked. It was like a cell phone, but a lot older. It was also attached to the wall.

She went over, tipped the garbage can over and stepped on it. She examined the telephone carefully. There were slots for the money. "I need money to make it work."

Boo checked her jeans and found she still had her left-over lunch money. A dollar bill and three dimes. She lifted the phone and read how to work it. She dropped the dime into the ten-cent slot and heard a dial tone.

She called home. She waited impatiently while the phone rang on the other end. She prayed that someone was there.

Brandon heard the phone ring and picked it up. "Hey, this is Brandon."

"Brandon, it's Boo."

"Boo, where are you?"

"With Cruella, I mean Chan Dana something. I don't remember her last name."

"Boo, where are you?"

"I don't know. We drove far."

"Think, Boo. What is it look like? Did you recognize anything?"

"We passed a town called Leaderful."

Chan Dana pounded on the door. "Open up, kid. Now"

"who's that?"

"Cruella. I gotta go. Tell Charlie to come and find me. Hurry."

"I'm coming, Cruella."

"Hurry it up, or I'll kill this kid out here."

Boo quietly put the phone back on the hook and opened the door."

"Sometimes it takes a while."

"Going get the directions."

"Sure, just don't and kill anyone."

~~~

"Boo! Boo, don't hang up." Brandon slammed down the phone and ran down to the barn where Charlie was tending the injured cow. It ran over to him and said, "Charlie. You called."

"When?"

"Just now. She said someone named Chan Dana got her. She thinks she's near a town called Leaderful."

"That's over towards Tennessee. Come on, we need to call the Sheriff and Dillon."

"There was pounding in the background and she said she had ago. Charlie, she said she was okay, just scared some."
~~~

Chapter 20

Chan Dana looked down at the device in her hand. She had finally gotten a location on Tanocka Burns. He was close, very close. She wanted to start immediately, but first there was the problem of gas.

She looked over at Boo, "where is this place we get the gas?"

"Leroy Masterson, that's the clerk you wanted to kill." Boo stopped talking and looked at Chan Dana. "Why do you want to kill everyone? Do you know how awful that is? The Sheriff would arrest you would put you in jail for the rest your life. Jail isn't a very nice place."

"How many times do I have to tell you to shut up? You keep up and you'll be next. Where is this place you find gas?"

"Leroy said there's a station about 3 miles down this road before you hit the highway. You just have to keep going until you see their sign. Cruella, I'm hungry. Did you get anything at the store?"

"You can wait. Eat this." She said throwing a bag at Boo.

"That's a doughnut. I mean real food. If I promise to be good and not give you a hard time, can we stop at a restaurant?"

Chan Dana was also hungry and the idea of another meal with what she now considered real food was tempting. "Let's get the gas first. We have to feed this machine."

Boo couldn't help but laugh. She had never thought about gassing up a car as feeding it.

"What's so funny?"

"Nothing, Cruella. There," Boo pointed to the gas on the left sign. "That's the gas station. You have to drive up and park next to the pump."

Chan Dana parked next to the pump as she was directed by Boo. She got out and looked at the gas pump. She had absolutely no idea how this worked. She decided to try to speak to it.

"Need gas for the machine."

Boo got out and walked over to Chan Dana. She would've tried to run, but knew that Chan Dana could easily outdistance her.

"You don't talk to it. You gotta go inside and pay and then they'll turn on the pump. Don't hurt the guy in there."

Chan Dana grabbed Boo by the shoulder. "Get moving." Boo stood next to Chan Dana. She looked down at her and asked, "how much money?"

Boo shrugged. "Twenty-two dollars."

Chan Dana growled at her and pulled out a wad of money from her pocket. She said, "which one?"

Boo took out a twenty and two one-dollar bills. She slapped them down on the counter and said, "pump number three."

They went outside and once again, Chan Dana stood in front of the gas pump. "Now what?"

"You don't know anything, do you? You take the hose off, press the button, and then you can fill the tank."

When Chan Dana looked confused, Boo took the hose from her. She pointed at the car and said, "open the gas tanks door."

Boo giggled when Chan Dana tried to pry open the little door. "Here, hold this."

She shoved the gas hose at her and went over to the car.

"There's a release somewhere in the car. It's new."

It took her a minute to find the release for the gas door and then she went back and took the hose from Chan Dana. She opened the lid and put the gas hose into it. She looked up at Chan Dana, "that's it."

After the gas tank was full, Boo told Chan Dana that she needed to eat some real food. The woman looked at her, she thought she would pull her hair out if she didn't get rid of this kid.

"Is that all you do is eat?"

Boo put her hands on her hips, "Look, Cruella, I don't know how it is where you come from, but here we eat at least three meals a day. If I don't eat, I'll get hypoglycemic." That was another word that she had learned from Dillon.

"What's that?"

"There won't be any sugar in my blood and I'll pass out right here on the concrete. It could happen. I got to eat six times a day."

Boo didn't think that that was how it worked, but she didn't have a problem lying to Cruella. She had heard Dillon use this word when he was explaining it to a patient.

Once again, Chan Dana grabbed Boo by the arm and threw her into the car.

~~~

"I think I found her." Jackson shouted. "Here, the tracker dog....."

"Connery?" Moose interrupted......"

"Okay, Connery, he indicates she's headed south."
~~~

Moose grimaced as he got up. "Let's go."

Dude held up a set of keys. "I'll drive."

They tracked Chan Dana all day before Moose had to stop.

"She's not that far away from us. With a little luck we'll catch up to them very soon."

"We should go on, Jackson."

"Until you fall over? Tomorrow, Bill. We all need to rest. Chan Dana will be waiting for us, she's not stupid. She has to know were following her."

"What about Boo? I don't want her hurt, and the longer she's with her there's a bigger chance of it."

Jackson actually thought that the little girl was already dead. Chan Dana didn't keep anyone around when she was on a search, or running. She was doing both. Boo would be a problem for her, one that she wouldn't hesitate to eliminate.

The next morning, Dude stopped for gas and asked about a woman who was traveling with a little girl.

"Treated that little girl mean. She didn't seem to know how to pump the gas in the car, or how to pay for it. The child had to show her."

"Happen to know where they were headed?"

"When out of here going south, headed out to Highway #72."

"Thank you. Appreciate your help."

Dude went back to the car. "She went south on Highway # 72. Thew man, inside is sure of it, and he said she had a little girl with her. I'm guessing that must be Boo."

"What does the tracker dog say?" Moose asked.

"It doesn't say anything. I don't think it's working."

"I guess we go south." Dude said.

~ ~ ~

Tanocka Burns knew that agent Mark Kona Lester was searching for him. He also knew that he would never find him. Tanocka Burns had left many misleading clues to throw Mark off of his trail. Right now, he was on a planet called, Amber Blue.

Amber Blue was a small planet that was discovered approximately five hundred years ago. It was several light-years away from Jupiter. It had been colonized three hundred years ago and had twelve different establish colonies. Each colony had over ten thousand residents. Men, women, and children all lived in harmony with each other. They would exchange the goods that they acquired with the and other communities.

Amber Blue was an underground establishment where everyone lived in the interior of the planet because the outside atmosphere was to hostile an environment to sustain any human life form. In the summers the constant winds blew hot and could reach over 130°. The summer months were short and only ran for six Earth months.

The planet had two suns, one red, one brown. In the winter months which ran for approximately ten earth months it went frigid with cold. Blue ice formed into mountains that took over the entire planet. The temperatures reached thirty below or colder.

In the summer, the red sun ran brilliantly hot and the brown son paled to a sickly beige. In the winter the brown sun became dominant, and the red sun would pale to a lukewarm pink.

The only thing that lived on the surface of the Amber Blue planet was a hideous creature that changed with the two seasons.

This creature was deadly, it could and would kill anything that moved into its path. The colonists never went to the surface without protection. They had developed a stunning device called a McMaster. If they would encounter the creatures, which they called, The Mac, it would temporarily incapacitate it. They would have exactly 6 minutes to flee to safety. Sometimes, six minutes was not enough.

On those rare occasions when the residents were forced to surface it was always in the beginning of the winter months. The Mac's seemed to be fewer and further spread out. No one knew where they would go, but there was a six-week period that was deemed the safest.

The colonists would gather blue glowing water from the surface that they needed to sustain their existence. It was their only water source, and the only time it could be harvested was within that six-week period otherwise it was just too dangerous.

At this time the water hadn't frozen solid and could be handled in large chunks which they took to a special room where it was left to melt. They would spend the entire six weeks gathering everything that was needed for the coming year. Below the surface the large holding tanks secured the water in an area on the east side of the compound.

The Mac, was seen in various sizes from a little larger than the average man to a huge creature. It was very powerful and even the smallest of them could easily kill a man.

The creature walked on two feet, but could run on all four. Dalton Everest, the leader of the Amber Blue society had heard The Mac described in many ways. It looked part human and part animal, it was described as a Goliath, a monster, and a devil. The truth was that it was neither human or animal, it was just some kind of a deformed freak. Dalton Everest explained that it was one of nature's mistakes. A mistake that would eat you.

The Mac could easily be seen because it was red on the right side and brown on the left. Dalton Everest thought there was some correlation between the two suns and the in the coloring of The Mac. The hair, or fur was long. The one thing they knew for sure was that it had an unsatisfied appetite when it was hungry.

The Mac ate yellow glowing plant life that grew in abundance on the north side of the planet. They only eat twice a month for an entire day. These were the days that were the safest for the transports to come and go. It had given them a six-hour window. Everything on Amber Blue took proper timing to make it work.

The debate about The Mac continued, some thought the coloring was too close to deny that everything was a coincidence. When the sun ran hot that part of The Mac glowed with it. In the winter when the sun ran cold, so did the brown color of the beast.

The Mac was more deadly in the winter months. It could be heard even in the underground. It screamed a savage wildcat sound that penetrated downward. Most of the colonists had gotten used to the screams and were no longer startled by them. The only time it as totally unnerving was when it echoed and seemed to flow throughout the different communities.

The planet, Amber Blue, was not very inviting and somewhat restrictive because you were literally trapped underground the entire time you were there.

Tamocka Burns had chosen it as a temporary solution to his problems. He knew he was being hunted not only by the Ataca League of Law Enforcement, A.K.A., agent Mark Kona Lester, but by Chan Dana Ray as well. She blamed him for her father's death.

Tamocka Burns was resting in one of the hostel units provided to visitors. He wondered why anyone would actually come here to visit. The damn planet was hostile.

The roar of The Mac floated across the hostel. That made his decision, it was time for him to leave. He couldn't stand the constant reminder of that shaky demon above them. Unlike the people who lived here on a regular basis he would never get used to it.

Amber Blue had three transports off of the planet a year. In a week he could catch a transport and go to platform #6 which wasn't more than a transportation station itself from there he could go to other planets. Once there he could use his stolen Sundowner and travel back to old earth. He felt he could effectively disappear in that time period. He had to make sure that he was on the transport.

Chapter 21

Boo was again tied to the bed post. This time it was in a motel called, the Little Stars. Cruella was off somewhere; she had been gone for a very long time. Boo had been working to get free, but it just wasn't going to happen. She had taken a knife from the Banana Jack restaurant they stopped at for lunch. She had hoped it would help her get free.

"That sure was a dumb name for a restaurant." She mumbled as she worked at slowing the ropes with the stolen knife. She soon realized that it just wasn't working. It was a butter knife and it wasn't sharp enough to go through the rope. She looked carefully at the knife.

"Maybe I could just stab Cruella with it and run."

She liked the idea, but knew that that wouldn't work either. She leaned back on the bed and thought about Charlie, Brandon, and her best friend, Connery. She desperately wanted to go home. She wanted Dillon to hold her so she wouldn't be afraid anymore. And Moose, her Moose, Cruella had killed him. She had seen it and couldn't get it out of her mind. She tried not to think about it because it made her cry. She closed her eyes, there was Moose with blood around him. She decided she couldn't cry for Moose anymore, now she had to be angry for him. Moose was her friend, and now he would be gone from her forever.

"I hope Jackson does find you, and I hope he puts you in jail forever and you get nothing to eat but bread and water for the rest your life."

The door opened and Cruella came in. Boo glared at her. Cruella didn't say a word, she took out her knife and cut the ropes holding Boo to the bed. She threw a bag at her. Boo didn't talk to her either, she grabbed the bag, opened it and looked in. It was another cheeseburger.

"Is this all you know how to order?" Boo asked as she struggled out of the ropes on her wrists. She looked down at her wrists, they were starting to bleed from the constant scraping of the ropes.

"Eat it. We have to leave."

Boo looked at her left wrist, it hurt and was oozing blood.

"I need some bandages and antiseptic." Antiseptic was another word that she had learned from Dillon.

"What are you talking about now?"

Boo held out her wrists. "The ropes are cutting me. You don't want me to get infected. That could be horrible. I could go foaming at the mouth. I could get hydrophobia or something."

This was another word from Dillon. She never thought that she would find them useful, but now she was really glad that she had listened to him.

"What is hydrophobia?"

"It's really bad." Boo said solemnly. "It's a bug and travels all through your body. It can make you crazy when it hit your brain and you go bite whatever's near you, and then you can get sick too." She shook her head. "You don't want that." She was beginning to like lying to Cruella. "We don't really want to mess with this. I should see a doctor."

Chan Dana didn't know this time well enough to know if that kid was telling her the truth. Too many things here were unfamiliar to her. The last thing she wanted was to have a crazy, foaming, biting kid on her hands. For the hundredth time she thought that she should just kill her and be done with it. Jackson was what stopped her.

"No doctor."

"Then we need to find a convenience store so I can get some bandages and antibiotic stuff."

Chan Dana was trying to decide if she should just kill her and dump her in the car trunk, or find the convenience store, whatever that was. This kid was trouble enough without some Hydro whatever getting into her. She grabbed Boo by the shoulder and pushed her toward the car.

"Get yourself in there." She said angrily.

Boo looked at her and then went into the back seat. Chan Dana got into the driver's seat and turned around her. "Listen up. I am tired of hauling you around. We will find this convenience store thing and get whatever, and then nothing more. I will tell you when to eat, and went to sleep. You better just better start walking softer around me. I'm tempted to find Jackson myself and get rid of you. Got it!" She shouted. "Do we understand each other?"

"Sure, Cruella, I understand. I have to go the bathroom."

"Sit on it." She said through gritted teeth.

Chapter 22

Tanocka Burns made arrangements to return to earth by transport. He couldn't stand this planet for one more minute. He didn't understand how they could colonize a planet with those monsters on the surface. Hiding was one thing, but being tortured by some hairy beast was another.

It was time to chance coming out of hiding. Once he got back to earth of his time he was going to transport back to earth of the past and hide there. He would find Chan Dana and eliminate that problem first. Instead of letting her try to kill him, or worse, incapacitated him so he couldn't fight. He was going to turn it all back on her. He would go after her, and then take care of agent Mark Kona Lester. Only then will he be free.

Tanocka Burns gathered what little he had and threw it into his backpack. The backpack was worn and had a hole in it, but it still worked good enough for him. He looked over at the platform clock, he had to be at the station within the hour. He would take the elevated to the transport station and wait for the actual transport plane which would take him off of this planet.

Tanocka Burns arrived at the elevated with fifteen minutes to spare. There were several other people waiting to also go to transport. A woman dressed in a blue uniform asked him for his papers. He handed her his paperwork, she looked at it and then at him. He was traveling under the name of Leroy Lee Wilson. He paid a lot for this identification and everything matched perfectly, his ID picture was current.

"Go to station 8. You will be taken to the surface and moved over to the transport where you will meet with the plane." She handed him his papers and moved on to the next person.

The platform took not only Tanocka Burns up to the surface, but the six others. There were three men, two women, and a very small boy. When they got to the surface the wind was howling and visibility was low. The woman with the child picked him up and held him close to her.

They were in a small square, three-sided station platform that offered some protection from the wind. It was covered on the three sides but left an opening in the front. They all moved to the back of the station to wait for the transport. They could hear it in the distance as it moved closer.

The transport was slowly descending onto the platform pad several hundred feet in front of them and was barely visible in the whipping wind. The transport came straight down, it's green and red landing lights flickering in circles.

Tanocka Burns saw something approaching out of the corner of his eye. It was coming from the north of the transport. The wind had started to blow faster moving quickly into swirling circles, visibility became even less. The planet was in its changing days from the summer sun which was becoming dull, to the winter sun which was brightening in color.

Tanocka Burns heard a low growl to his left and turned in time to glimpse a large shape. It was just a glimpse of something dark, a blur in the wind, nothing more than a vague indication of what he thought might have been, the Mac. He knew that they were deadly and had very large teeth, and they were fast. You couldn't outrun them. He didn't understand why they would be here, at this time. They were supposed to be on the other side of the planet, getting their nutrition for the next six hours. They were supposed to have a six-hour leeway before they became active again. The last thing they were supposed to be was around the compound.

Tanocka Burns looked over at the other people on the platform, they either didn't see what he did, or they were oblivious to it. He reached into his coat and felt his gun to reassure himself. He rubbed his eyes and stared into the murky air beyond him. He listened intently for any sound.

Just beyond the station, the transport plane continued to descend onto the platform. He saw a flash of brown appearing in the landing lights from the transport.

He shook his head. "It's so darn hard to see them."

Tanocka Burns searched his pockets and found the Google glasses he always kept there. He put them on, but they were of little help. The air was moving swiftly kicking up a murky cloud and visibility was compromised.

Then he heard it. It was unmistakably the wildcat scream that came right before a Mac attack. The Mac was huge, it stood over 8 feet tall and with it were several smaller ones that were barely visible.

The two creatures moved forward with a smaller one, they came from both sides. The larger of them came from the front while a third creature, and then a fourth circled the sides of the station. They had effectively surrounded the people on the station's platform.

Tanocka Burns looked for a way out, but all the escape routes had been blocked by these creatures. The only way to get out was to go back to the underground. He knew the authorities were aware of the situation because there was an observation camera just above them.

The woman with the child ran to the corner of the station, flipped open the emergency alert and press the large button. Nothing happened. She started to pound on the door screaming as loud as she could. The swift moving wind drowned out the pleads for help. One of the men went over to her and attempted to help her while the other two, and the remaining woman stood their ground and didn't move. There was nowhere to go.

The growling became louder over the noise of the wind and the pounding of running feet. The Mac creatures were attacking.

Tanocka Burns crouched down and aimed his gun in the direction of the roaring noises. He waited. Suddenly, two red eyes glowed through the gloom. Tanocka Burns took careful aim and pulled the trigger. They heard the inhuman roar of the Mac as it struck out grabbing one of the men from the platform station.

The woman clutched her child to her and screamed beating furiously at the door. The child also started to scream. Another Mac lumbered onto the station platform tweaking its tail striking the man and woman hovering in the farthest corner. They vanished from sight.

Tanocka Burns yelled for the other men to help him. He stood frozen next to the screaming woman and child. In front of them, Tanocka Burns could see the transport attempting to lift off of the planet surface. Several of the Macs pounced at it. He saw the pale, terror-stricken faces of the pilot and copilot right before the transport was pushed over onto its side. The four Macs that attacked it started pounding on the transport body. They actually rolled the big plane back and forth between them like they were playing some type of game with it. From inside of the plane shouts and screams could be heard over the rushing wind. Tanocka Burns closed his eyes, he knew that the transport plane was doomed. He took out the second gun he had in his jacket and prepared himself to die.

Suddenly, the door on the platform snapped open. The screaming woman threw her child into the small transport elevator and attempted to jump in after him. She wasn't fast enough and the door snapped close crushing her. The only thing left on this side of the door were her legs. The remaining man on the platform with Tanocka Burns screamed as a Mac bit down on him.

Tanocka Burns slowly backed up to the transport door as three more Max's approached him. If he was going to die, he would go down fighting. He crouched down onto one knee and fired the rest of his bullets into the closest Mac. He dropped that gun and aimed his other pistol at the approaching Mac. He waited for it to get closer before he emptied his gun into it.

After the attack of the Macs was over, they slowly moved off carrying the body of Tanocka Burns with them.

Chapter 23

Boo woke to someone speaking. She lay quiet on the bed, the ropes were burning her wrists, but she ignored it and try to listen to what was being said. Did Chan Dana have someone there with her? The room was still dark, it was still night, she looked over at the clock on the dresser next to the bed. It was four in the morning. She squinted her eyes to see if she could see another shape in the bed next to Chan Dana. She was sitting straight up on the side of the bed and it was her who was talking.

Boo carefully rolled to her side, closed her eyes and attempted to hear what was being said, and to whom. There was a steady stream of conversation, one voice was definitely Chan Dana's, but the other one she didn't recognize. She looked harder into the dark, but couldn't see anyone except Chan Dana.

A deep voice that sounded like a man said, "I'm telling you; you have to get rid of the kid. She's a threat to you. She slows you down."

"It may be the only way that I can get Jackson to come to me, and then I'll have the advantage."

"That may be true, but you have to weigh if the cost is worth it. This kid can identify you. This kid has been nothing but a pain in the ass. Maybe it would be better if you sought out Jackson." The man said. "Go after him. Kill him."

"I still think she may be useful. Trust me, I would not take her with me if I thought otherwise."

"You have to hurry because I fear that your time is running out."

"Why would you say that?"

"The longer you stay on this planet, in this time the more dangerous it becomes for you."

"It's the only thing I can do to save you."

"Have you ever thought that perhaps I'm beyond saving?"

"Don't say that, father, you are the future, our future, without you I cannot take over the world."

Boo couldn't believe what she was hearing. There was no one there, and Cruella was holding a conversation as if there was. There were definitely two different voices, one was Cruella's, and the other sounded like a man. Boo didn't know how that could be. She was sure that there was only Cruella and herself in the room. She wondered if she should call out to her, but decided to listen for a little while longer and maybe she could learn something that would be helpful to her.

"All right then, father. I am tired and require sleep. We will talk again."

Cruella got up and turned on the light. Boo quickly closed her eyes and pretended to be asleep. The last thing she wanted her to know was that she had heard her conversation with her father? How could she be talking to her father when there wasn't anyone there? She would ask Cruella tomorrow about her father, but she knew that she would have to be very careful. She wanted to go home.

She wanted to be with Dillon, Charlie and Brandon. She missed Connery and wished he was here with her. Tears slipped down her face as she thought that she may never see them again. She knew that Cruella was dangerous. She yanked on the rope and screamed silently. She was no longer going to cry, she was mad, madder than she had ever been in her life. She had to find a way to get away from Cruella. Charlie had always told her when she was in trouble to think. Remain calm and see if there was a way out of whatever trouble she was in. She would think all night if she had to and she would find a way out of this. She knew that everyone would be looking for her so maybe she could leave them help. She would start tomorrow.

~~~

Chan Dana cut the ropes on Boo's wrists. Boo rubbed them, they hurt and the left one was bleeding. On the table a bag sat. Cruella pointed to it.

"Eat. We need to get moving."

"Where exactly are we going?"

"None of your business."

"Okay, but are you sure you know the way?"

"Eat."

Boo sat down and opened the bag. Inside was an egg sandwich with a cup of coffee. "Cruella, I'm nine years old, I don't drink coffee."

"The man said it comes with it."

Boo looked at the cup in her hand and then at Cruella. She cleared her throat and said, "kids don't drink coffee. We drink milk. If I was home, the home you stole me from, Brandon would milk our cow, Mildred."

"Cow?"

"I suppose you don't know what a cow is either?"

"I've heard of one, but have never seen one. We do not have cows in the future."
~~~

"That's what Moose said." Boo thought about Moose and wanted to cry. She held back because she wouldn't cry in front of Cruella. She was nothing but an old witch."

"Hurry up and finish that, we need to leave."

Boo finished her biscuit and smiled. She pointed to the room across from the bed. "I have to go to the bathroom before we can leave."

"We don't have time."

"Okay, if you want to stop in fifteen minutes."

"Go, and make it fast."

Boo closed the bathroom door and ran the water in the sink. She placed her wrist under the water. It was so sore and it made it feel better. It relieved some of the sting. She left the water running and searched through the drawers of the vanity. In the bottom drawer she heard something roll when she opened it. She reached in and pulled out a round tube.

"Lipstick."

Boo grinned and opened it up. She looked over at the mirror and smiled. She put the toilet seat down, hopped up on it and then onto the vanity. She opened the lipstick and began writing on the mirror.

She wrote:

I'm kidnapped.

Going south with Cruella.

Call my brother Charlie.

800-555-6331

Boo jumped down and started for the door, she stopped and went back and flush the toilet. She turned off the water and turned out the light. She shoved the lipstick deep inti her pocket. When she stepped out of the bathroom, Cruella was waiting.

Boo hoped she wouldn't go in and discover the writing on the mirror. "I'm ready." She called.

Chan Dana pushed her towards the door and out of the room. They went over to the car and she opened the door

"Get in."

Boo started to get in the car, but stopped and turned to Cruella.

"Just where are we going? All we seem to do is drive around. It's becoming very tiring."

"It's none of your business. Get in before I break your little neck for you."

"Okay, but you don't have to be so nasty and hateful. Do you even know where were going?"

"Yes. I have a tracking dog."

Boo was confused. She looked around, but all she saw was a road, the motel, bunch of trees, and a few people across the street, no dog. She didn't get it. They never had a dog with them.

"You don't have a dog. I haven't seen one since we left the farm."

Chan Dana held out a mechanical device. "It's right here."

Boo looked carefully at the device in Cruella's hand. It was small, kind of a green in color, and had some kind of blank screen on it. She thought maybe it was some kind of computer.

Boo gave Cruella a disgusted look, "that is not a dog. A dog is real, that's some kind of a machine."

"That is a tracking dog of my time. It is very real."

"No, something real is living, breathing, and warm. Connery is a dog, he's all of that, yours is nothing but a machine."

Chan Dana wanted to kill this kid. All she did was argue with her. She gritted her teeth.

"Listen carefully. Get in the car and keep your mouth shut, or I will tie you up, and dump you in the truck."

"Okay. I'm getting in. Chill, Cruella."

Chapter 24

Jackson tracked Chan Dana to the motel she and Boo spent the night in. A young man, no older than twenty was sitting in the chair behind the desk half-asleep. Jackson hit the counter with his hand. The kid jumped up almost falling off of the chair.

Jackson, Moose, and Dude stood across from him. Dude stepped forward. "Let me do this." He looked carefully at the kid. The fact that he didn't want to be here was written all over his face. Dude thought this was going to be easy.

"That your bike out front?"

"Yeah."

"Really nice bike."

"Yeah, but I'm still restoring it. Got a way to go."

"I got fifty bucks in my pocket that will be yours if you tell me about the woman and the little girl that spent the night here."

"Weird woman. Cute little kid."

"That sounds about right."

"They stayed in 114. She paid cash which was somewhat unusual."

"Fifty bucks for the key. We won't be long."

The kid turned around, scanned the computer and handed Dude the key card. "Knock yourself out."

Dude placed the fifty dollars on the counter. "Nice doing business with you."

They went down to room 114. Dude opened the door. He stepped back as Jackson and Moose entered. Once inside he closed the door and they started to search the room. Dude said he had to use the bathroom. He stopped dead in his tracks when he saw the message on the mirror. He stepped over to the door and called, "Jackson, Bill, Boo left us a message."

The three men stood in front of the mirror and read the message for the fourth time.

Moose said sadly. "She thinks I'm dead."

"Well," Jackson said. "We're going to have to find her and show her that you're very much alive."

"South." Dude said pointing to the mirror. "South could be anywhere."

"She's heading for Kentucky."

"Why Kentucky?"

Because that was the last place Tanocka Burns was reported at. She'll follow him because she wants him dead more than she wants me and Bill dead."

"Kentucky is a big state."

"Chan Dana's one flaw in her thinking is that she goes in a direct line. She doesn't know we are after her, so she won't even think about deviating from that and try to lose us. Tanocka Burns is in Bowling Green, Kentucky."

Dude laughed. "Well, at least that narrows it down some."

"What do we know about Bowling Green?" Bill asked.

Dude shrugged. "It's in southern Kentucky. Got a great Corvette Museum, lots of classic cars and prototypes in there. They also have a museum that is devoted entirely to the Civil War. It also has a lot of colleges and universities. It's a pretty big city."

"Stop." Jackson said. "What we need to concentrate on is where there would be a good place to hide for a while."

"Are we going into hiding?" Dude asked.

"No, but Tanocka Burns will be in hiding. How do you know so much about Bowling Green, Kentucky?"

"I used to live there. Let me think about it for a minute."

Dude sat down in the chair that Boo had occupied hours earlier. "I got it. I got the best place ever. The perfect place to hide. The Lost River Caves.

"What is that? And where is that?"

"It's in Bowling Green. The Lost River Caves, yeah, that's it. There used to be an actual underground boat tour you could take, even a walking tour. There's about 60 acres of wooded trails up there. It's called the Lost River because the source of the river has never really been discovered. The Native Americans lived in the Lost River caves way back. They used it for shelter, food, and water. There are a lot places to hide out in there. A lot of places where no one would go. We used to run around there as kids. I think it's been closed up for a while.

The water in the cave is about 25 feet deep in most places, but there are some spots where its low enough that makes it easy to cross. Inside the Lost River is a passageway called the Blue Hole. Years ago, it was listed in Ripley's believe it or not, it is the shortest, deepest river in the whole world.

The Blue Hole is 437 feet deep while the river is only 2 feet long. Cave floors are riddled with limestone.

The Pueblo Indians lived there about ten thousand years ago. The cave has drinkable water and offered them shelter in the winter months.

Cave was used during the Civil War too, by both the North and the South. The Confederates occupied it from 1861 to 1862. Union soldiers used it to camp after they took it over in eighteen sixty-two, I think around March of that year. If you go in deep enough their names written on the cave walls. Soldiers wrote the ranks and the outfits that they served in. Bullets from the Union Army source discovered within some of the cave chambers.

It's also told that the outlaw Jesse James hid in the caverns of the cave. Nobody knows for sure if that's true. Cave has hit hard times too. A while back there was a nightclub called, The Cavern Nightclub, but that ended sometime in the 1960s.

Early 1986 would bring more hardship to the Lost River when it was neglected and literally became a garbage dump. Many things were dumped at the site, old refrigerators, stoves, washing machines, old tires, and an assortment of other garbage.

In nineteen ninety, nonprofit organization would clean up the site. The cave would be reopened to the public in nineteen ninety-seven. But this was all in the future.

When Chan Dana and Boo arrived the Lost River Cave was still in a state of destruction. What was once a beautiful area was little more than the place to dump things now. That wouldn't stop it from being a perfect hiding place."

Dude looked at Jackson. "There are many places you can go not be discovered in there, but I'd be guessing where he would be."

Jackson shook his head knowingly. "I still think Chan Dana will go there."

"How can, you be sure?"

"Because she has a tracker dog and that's where it's leading both of us."

Chapter 25

Chan Dana was unaware of Tanocka Burns death. She was following the trail that he had left behind and this is where the tracking dog was taking her. Soon she would be eliminating Tanocka Burns, and then it was Jackson's turn.

"They will all die. Tanocka Burns, Jackson, and Bill. Gone father."

Boo looked around the car. They were alone. There was no father, just her and Cruella. The woman was bat crazy. She was talking to someone who wasn't even there.

"Who are you talking to?"

Cruella looked in the rearview mirror at Boo. She sneered at her, "no one. Shut up."

"You said father. Where is your father?"

"Dead."

"Mine too. He died when I was four."

"Mine was murdered by the authorities. Tanocka Burns, Jackson Raymond Garcia, and Bill Trader were responsible and now they must die."

"You using me to get to this man Jackson?"

"I've already killed Bill Trader, the one that you call Moose. Jackson will come right after Tanocka Burns."

"The Sheriff will put you in jail forever because you killed my Moose."

"You're not going to tell anyone anything so I won't be put in jail. Now shut up and leave me alone so that I can drive."

Boo sat back on the seat. Her wrists burned and hurt from the constantly being tied up. She felt a cold chill go through her body. She finally understood that this woman would kill her. She would only use her until she was no longer valuable to her and then she would kill her as fast as she did Moose.

"Do you want to eat? I am hungry."

"Sure, Cruella, there was a sign back there it said, 'Cocci River Diner.' It's off of the next exit."

Chan Dana turned off at the next exit. The signs pointed to where the diner was. She parked in the parking lot and turned to Boo.

"You will behave or the next time you'll be in the trunk."

Boo held out her hands. "It's going to look funny if I'm eating with my hands tied up."

Chan Dana cut the ropes and waved the knife in Boo's face. "No funny business."

When they got into the restaurant they were seated at the counter because every table was occupied.

Boo took the menu and studied it. She looked over at Cruella, she looked normal enough. Black hair, brown eyes, she wasn't too ugly. She seemed to be of average height, maybe 5 foot six, kind of the skinny side. No one would suspect that she was a witch.

"Where exactly are we going, Cruella?"

"Bowling Green, Kentucky."

"Is that where Jackson will be?"

"No, he will not be there, but he will follow us."

A middle-aged woman came over to the counter. She smiled down at Boo and asked, "what will it be?"

Cruella shook her head as she tried to study the menu. Boo looked at her and said, "I'll order."

"All right little Miss, what will you and your friend here have?"

"She's not my friend. She's a kidnapper. I'll have a cheeseburger, fries, and a chocolate shake. Cruella will have a tuna fish sandwich, and a cup of coffee."

"Coming right up."

Lorna Neville looked back at Boo. She was sure that she had heard her correctly. The child said the woman next to her was a kidnapper, but did that mean that she was kidnapped by this woman?

Lorna had a heap of her own problems to worry about, including an abusive boyfriend that she was trying to get away from. She thought about him, it had started out good, but he quickly lost his job, started drinking, and then took it all out on her. She had been with Anton Lester a little over two years and she decided she was through. She is going to tell them he had to leave.... Tonight!

Lorna decided that she would call the police if she had to get away from Anton. She looked back at the child again and thought she would call the police about her and the woman after she resolved her own problem. It was all she could think about right now, how to get rid of Anton.

Lorna looked at Boo again and thought, kids lie. Maybe this was her mother and she was mad at her for some reason. She didn't know, this kid didn't look like one that was a liar.

When Chan Dana and Boo left, Lorna noted the license plate number on her car. It was a Chevy, 1982, plate number, C64733WD. She wrote it on her pad. She gave Boo another thought and decided that she didn't want to wait, waiting may be a problem for the child. She would report it to the Sheriff right now.

Lorna picked up the receiver on the phone when Stella, her coworker, called out to her.

"Mr. wonderful is on the phone in the office. He sounds really pissed."

Lorna groaned, put the diner phone down and went to the office in the back of the restaurant. She looked down at the telephone like it would jump up and bite her.

"What Anton? I'm at work. Remember the rent. Someone has to pay it, so I have to work."

"Relax, Baby. I just called to tell you that I got a job at Anderson's auto repair. I start the job tomorrow, pays really good so will have no more worries."

"You better not lose this job, Anton."

"I won't. When are you coming home?"

"Probably around seven. I'm going to cash my check at the bank and then I'm coming straight home."

"Okay. I'll have dinner ready."

"Your cooking?"

"Sure, were going to celebrate."

Stella opened the door. "Were swamped."

"Coming."

"I've got to go. See you later."

Lorna hung up and hurried to help Stella. She completely forgot about Boo. After she went to the bank to cash her check, Lorna remembered about the little girl. She would call the sheriff as soon as she got home.

Lorna never called the sheriff about Boo when she walked into her apartment she was struck from behind. The blow hit the back of her head causing a severe concussion with a brain bleed. She would live for six minutes.

Anton stood over her with a baseball bat in his hand. He reached down and took her purse. He rummaged through the purse until he found the money, he threw the purse away from him.

"Sorry, but I'm hurting. I'll come back later for you. Got the perfect place to let you rest, for eternity. I'm going for a well needed drink or two. Later, Babe."

Anton left and went to his favorite bar, 'the Randy Brandy'. He was there for several hours before the police arrested him for Lorna's murder.

In Anton's haste to get to the bar, he failed to close the apartment door. Joanna King came home from work and saw Lorna's body in the doorway.

Chapter 26

Three hours later, Chan Dana drove into Bowling Green, Kentucky. Now all she had to do was find this Lost River. She turned to Boo, "how do we find out about this Lost River?"

"How would I know. I've never been in Kentucky before. If I was home and had my books, we could look it up, but you went and stole me and I don't have them with me."

"Get in the car and keep your mouth shut. You say one more thing about being kidnapped you'll spend your time in the trunk."

"Okay. Okay. It just slipped out."

"Don't let it happen again."

Boo looked around and pointed to a store. "Let's go in here."

"What is that place?"

"I think it's some kind of variety store."

"What is that?"

"It's a story that has all kinds of stuff in it."

"We don't need stuff, we need information."

"I'll ask." Boo said as she opened the door.

Jason Lee Thompson stood behind an old wooden counter. Boo spotted him and went over. "Hey, I'm Boo."

"Well, hey there Boo. I 'm Mason Lee."

"I like your name."

"Thank you. Boo is a pretty unusual name for a little girl."

"My real name is Allison Crawford, but I don't use it much." Her green eyes twinkled. "I live in Tustin, Georgia."

"Enough." Chan Dana said jerking her back towards her. "Ask him."

"Miss Boo, who exactly is this?"

She pointed at Chan Dana. "That's Cruella. She's always in a hurry. Could you tell me where the Lost River would be?"

"Sure can, but you don't want to go there. It used to be really nice, but there isn't much more than a junkyard. It was a nightclub once, it was pretty good back then now, it's not a place for little girls."

"We need to go there." Chan Dana said.

"Why would that be?"

"Doesn't concern you."

Boo didn't like the way this was going. She didn't trust Cruella; she was afraid that she would she would hurt this man. She had to get her outta here.

"Please, sir, everything will be okay. Could you just give me directions?"

Mason Lee reluctantly told Boo how to get to the Lost River."

"Y'all be careful." He called after her.

She turned around smiled and waved. "I will. Thank you."

After Chan Dana and Boo left, Mason Lee went to get the newspaper. He felt something was not right. He had seen that little girl before. He took all of the copies from last week and sat down with the Bowling Green daily news.

"There is something familiar about that child."

He carefully went through each day's paper until he found the article that he had been searching for. On page two, staring at him was a picture of Boo. He opened the paper and spread it out on the desk so that he could read the article.

It read,

Missing child from Tustin, Georgia. He quickly scanned the entire article for the information he was seeking. After he found it, he went to the telephone and called the Tustin Sheriff's office.

~~~

Jackson, Moose, and Dude arrived in Bowling Green the same day as Chan Dana did, but by the time they got there it was late evening.

"Now what?" Dude asked.

"We're very close. I can feel it. We need to find out where this Lost River is at. That seems to be the key to most of this."

"Okay, let's go find a gas station."

~~~

Chan Dana drove as close as she could to the Lost River area. Boo looked up into the darkening sky. It looked like it might rain. She glanced over at Chan Dana. "I sure don't see a river, lost or otherwise."

"Get out. We walk from here."

Chan Dana was getting anxious because all she wanted to do was find Tanocka Banks, kill him, and then get Jackson. She looked over at Boo. She sneered, "I can't wait for to be your turn."

"What does that mean?"

"Never mind. Get moving."

"Where?"

"Through there. What are all of these things?"

Boo looked around at the discarded washing machines, dryers, refrigerators, old tires, and just about anything else you can think of. "People's junk. They shouldn't do this."

"Who cares. Move it."

Boo carefully picked her way through all the junk people had dumped there. She tripped over a broken toilet and fell, she felt it cut her hand. She yelped.

"What's wrong?" Cruella yelled and backtracked to where Boo was sitting on the ground. She looked down at her and said, "get up."

Boo got up slowly. "I cut my hand."

"So what."

"It's bleeding."

"I don't care. We need to find Tanocka Banks, and he's in those.............. What did you call them?"

Boo had taken the handkerchief that she always carried in her pocket and wrapped her hand. "Caves. They are called caves. There could be a lot of different places to hide in there. Caves have a lot of hiding places in them."

"The tracking dog will find him."

"We could get lost in there."

"I will not get lost."

"You ever been in a cave before?"

"No."

"I have. Charlie took me into one. There, big and............" She stood for a moment and thought for the right word. When it came to her, she said, "Complicated."

Are you trying to stall me again?"

"Boo stomped over to Chan Dana. "Fine. Let's go."

They had to walk through the mountain of junk that had been dumped from the mouth of the cave to what had once been the parking lot. The junk was heaped everywhere and they had to wind in and out of it.

Finally, after dodging through all of the junk they reach the mouth of the cave, Boo looked into it and saw what she thought would be the Lost River. The entranceway was huge. Cruella and Boo made their way over to the river's edge. The water looked deep and extremely dark.

"This isn't going to work Cruella."

"Why? We have time to find Tanocka Burns."

"Look how dark it is in here. We going much further we won't be able to see anything at all. That's how caves are, dark, damp, and scary."

Chan Dana turned to Boo and slapped her across the face. She fell to the ground. Boo was surprised more than anything, she really didn't expect her to hit her again.

Cruella stood over her. "You knew this. Another delay." She hissed at her. "We will go on."

Boo rubbed her cheek. "We need flashlights."

Chan Dana grabbed Boo by the shoulder and dragged her back over to the car. She pointed at it. "You have a choice. Car or trunk."

"Car."

Chan Dana drove back to Mason Lee Thompson's variety store. "Get out. We're going to get flashlights and then were gone from here. No stalling. No talking to the man in there or I'll kill him. Have you got it?"

"Got it."

Boo went over to Mr. Thompson and smile. "I need some flashlights. Not little ones. Ones with a big, far beam."

"Why would a little one like you need with the far beamed flashlight?" Mason Lee asked as he turned from the counter to rummage on a shelf behind him.

Boo felt Cruella stiffen and growl next to her. That was the only way she could explain it…. The witch growled at her.

"Ghost stories. A bunch of us kids are spending the night together and will be telling ghost stories. It's scarier in the dark with flashlights."

"Guess we did the same when I was a kid. How many do you need?"

"There's four of us. Don't forget the batteries."

Chapter 27

Dude came back to the car after talking to the gas station attendant. "It's not far from here. It's getting late, what do you want to do? It will be really dark up there. We're going need some type of lighting."

"What kind?"

"Lanterns, flashlights, that kind of thing. We'll have to find a hardware store."

"We're so close." Jackson said. "She's probably already here. It's almost like I can feel her."

Dude thought for a moment. "It will be hard to go in at night. We could find that hardware store, get a room for the night, and start first thing in the morning."

"I'm afraid Dude is right." Moose said. "In the daylight we will be able to see what's in front of us, and following behind us. Chan Dana isn't stupid and she won't be trying it in the dark either."

~~~

Chan Dana told Boo to get out of the car. Boo's hands were once again tied in front of her. She got out and Chan Dana grabbed her by the collar, she dragged her to the back of the car, opened the trunk and threw her in.

Boo tried to scream but Cruella had slapped duct tape across her mouth. Chan Dana slammed the trunk lid down. "If you know what's good for you, you'll be quiet in there or you'll regret it. If you don't keep quiet you will be riding in the trunk permanently."

~~~

Boo hated being confined in small places. It terrified her and she gasped for air. Not only was this small, but it was also dark. A double whammy. She could smell the rubber from the spare tire and it nauseated her. There was also an oily smell of some kind.

The worst thing was that she could smell her own fear. She shut her eyes tight and tried to think of something else. She thought of her dog, Connery.

Chan Dana got back into the driver seat and pulled the car into a darkened area behind several business establishments. She made sure that she was in the shadows before she got out and walked down the alleyway looking at all the doors. She finally decided on 'Chuck's Market Place.' She grinned, this would be easy and she needed money.

Chan Dana tried the door, it was locked. She simply took out a small tool called a BC 312. It took all of ten seconds to gain entry.

She laughed. "Works every time."

Chan Dana found herself in some type of a room that was loaded with all kinds of extra products that the store sold. She wasn't interested in the store's goods, what she needed was more of these times currency.

Chan Dana observed every store that they had gone into in the past. The money of the time was kept in a little drawer behind the counter. There was also something called a credit card, but she not only didn't have one, she didn't understand how they worked. They were worthless to her. She would stick to what is considered real money. She boldly walked through the room and out into the main store. There was a small woman locking the front door to the store.

Chan Dana called out to her. "Are you alone?"

The woman turned; she was startled by the voice because she thought the store was vacant.

"Oh dear, I didn't mean to lock you in. Please, come to the front of the store and I'll open the door for you."

Mrs. Helen Reynolds was sixty-nine years old, a widow for four years. She wasn't working because she wanted to, it was because she needed to supplement her income. She just didn't receive enough Social Security to live on. Her beloved husband, James, had been sick for several years and their modest savings was depleted quickly.

While Helen was waiting for the strange woman to come to the front door, she reflected that her feet hurt and she had a headache coming on, she was in a hurry. All she wanted was for this woman to leave so she could do the days banking and then deposit IT. After that was done, she could go home to her recliner and her television.

"I cannot leave." Chan Dana said. "I need money which I want you to provide."

"You're robbing me?"

"Yes, and you must hurry. I am in a hurry. There is no time to waste."

Helen marched over to Chan Dana. "I'm so sorry but I can't help you. Please leave immediately."

Chan Dana shot Helen Reynolds in the chest with the stolen revolver. She was dead before she hit the floor. Chan Dana calmly went behind the counter and looked for the place where the money was kept. She found over two thousand dollars waiting to be deposited into the bank.

Chan Dana left the store the way she came in. When she got to the car, she decided to leave Boo in the trunk. She drove until she found a familiar sight, the Greenway Motel. To her all of the motels looked alike and had the same basic needs for sleep which was all she was interested in.

Chan Dana parked the car and went around to the trunk. She opened it and gave Boo an evil smile. After she let her out of the trunk and untied her, they secured a room for the night.

"That was mean, Cruella. Mean and nasty."

"You deserved it."

"I'm hungry."

"Again?"

"That's what happens when you get locked up in a dark, smelly, trunk. Let's order pizza."

"What is pizza?"

"Food, Cruella. You'll like it."

Boo found a Book in the drawer with all kinds of food advertisements and it. She searched through it and picked out one called, Marco's pizza.

Chan Dana had never had a pizza before. She watched as Boo ate with her fingers. She followed her lead. At the first bite she was surprised at how good it was. She looked over at Boo, "I really like the food here."

"Yeah, well, you won't like jail food, all they give you is bologna sandwiches."

Boo found herself once again tied to the bed. Cruella was sound asleep on the other bed. While Boo worked on the rope she thought about tomorrow. They would be going to the caves to look for this Tanocka guy. Cruella was going to kill him. It seemed to be the only thing on her mind, killing. It she was understanding it right that would stop Cruella's father's death. That's what she had told her, but it really didn't make any sense to her. How could killing this man today prevent the death of Peter Rippen Ray hundreds of years from now? Maybe someone else would just come along and get him. Maybe he would die anyway. Charlie always said you can't change history. All of this from the future stuff confused her, so she put it out of her mind.

After Boo spent an hour trying to get free from the ropes she gave up because it just wasn't going to happen. All she accomplished was making her wrists hurt worse. They were bleeding and raw. The cut on her hand also hurt.

Suddenly, Chan Dana sat up on the edge of the bed. Boo scrunch down in the bed so that she couldn't be seen. It was time for the Cruella show.

Cruella would spend the next hour talking to her nonexistent father. The first few times it happened it actually scared her, but now Boo was used to it. The conversations (Cruella seemed to play both parts) were getting old and boring. It was always the same thing.

I'll save you father. I am so close, tomorrow we go to these caves where Tanocka Burns is hiding and I will make sure that he dies.

Boo rolled over and tuned her out. She hoped this Tanocka guy either wasn't there, or they wouldn't be able to find him. She so tired, and all she wanted to do was go home.

Boo was startled awake when Chan Dana shook her violently. "Get moving." She leaned down and cut the ropes.

Boo didn't say a word to her, she got up and went into the bathroom. She was surprised when she looked in the mirror. The reflection showed a large purple and black bruise on the left side of her face. This is where Cruella hit her. She also had the starting of a black eye. Gingerly, she touched her eye, it hurt. She slowly raised her arms and looked at her wrists, they were red and raw, a lot of the skin was broken. She went over to the sink, turned on the faucet and held her wrists under the cool water.

"I've got to get away from this witch."

An hour later they were back at the caves. Jackson, Moose, and Dude were not far behind them.

Chan Dana and Boo were once again picking their way through all the junk. The only difference was that they could see it much better in the daylight. Once they made it through all of the debris they were at the entrance of the cave.

The last thing Boo wanted was to go inside this darkened cave. She hesitated at the entrance. Cruella snarled at her, "get yourself moving."

Not only did Boo not want to be here, but she didn't feel good. Her head hurt and pounded with every step she took. She was running a high fever from the infected hand and her raw wrists. She wanted to go home, crawl in her own bed, with Connery, and stay there for at least a week.

Chan Dana shoved the little girl. "Keep moving."

"Okay, okay Cruella. These caves aren't going anywhere. They've been here for thousands of years."

They weren't very far in the cave before it turned dark. Once they left the entranceway there was very little light. Boo turned on the flashlight, eerie shadows bounced all around her. She turned back to Cruella who was even scarier in the dark.

"Which way?"

Chan Dana looked at her tracker dog. She had it set to find Tanocka Burns, but for some reason it wasn't registering properly. The signal seemed to be bouncing all over the place. She had to make an educated guess.

"Go straight."

Boo looked at her with disgust. "If we go straight, we will be walking right into the river. What else have you got?"

Chan Dana pushed her again. "Go left into that junction."

"Talk about stranger danger." Boo mumbled. "They need to put your picture on it, and then title it, the stranger at my side. Beware!"

"What are you talking about?"

"Nothing."

Chapter 28

As Chan Dana and Boo moved through the cave, Jackson, Moose, and Dude were entering the mouth of it. Dude cautiously looked inside, "it's pretty dark in there."

"That's why we brought the light."

"I don't like the dark."

Moose turned to Dude and smiled, "you can stay here. You helped us enough, more than we should have asked. It could be extremely dangerous from here."

"No, I said I would do this, I just don't like the dark."

"After the destruction of most of earth we lived in the underground. It was hard at first, but you used to it really fast. It was always dark down there."

Jackson had ventured into the entranceway. He looked around carefully and then down at the ground. He found footprints in the sandy area next to the river.

"They've been here. Bill come and look at this."

Moose went over to where Jackson was kneeling down. "Two sets of footprints. One is a child."

"We need to hurry."

~~~

"Which Way, Cruella?"

"The tracking dog has stopped." Chan Dana slowly turned around the entire area of the cave. "Jackson." She whispered.
~~~

"What about him?"

"He's here. Now, I can finally take care of him."

Boo screamed as loud as she could, "Jackson, run."

In one swift motion Boo turned and ran jumping into the river. She was an excellent swimmer, something that Charlie had insisted on after she almost drowned in the Red Spool Pond. She dived underneath the water just as Cruella shot at her. Boo thought that she actually felt the bullet move past her in the water. She swam underneath the water until she couldn't hold her breath anymore. When she surfaced, she discovered that she was alone. There was no sign of Cruella. She looked around for a good place to get out of the water.

Once Boo had pulled herself out of the water she started to edge back to where she had last seen Cruella. She didn't know Jackson, but she figured he was one of the good guys. If she could she would warn him again. She was scared, more frightened than she had ever been in her life, but she also knew that she couldn't back away, she had to do this.

Boo stayed in the shadows of the cave, close to the wall. She heard running water and moved over to an overhang. It led into a huge area enclosed by a series of walls. It looked like a hollowed-out area adjacent to the main cave. Inside was a huge waterfall that flowed down and back into the river. The walls were light pinkish in color with brown streaks running all through them.

Boo heard Cruella scream and moved closer. She wondered what she was screaming about, but didn't really care. She waited, but she didn't hear anything more except the roar of the waterfall. She had to get out, but the way out was ahead and it was blocked by Cruella. She squinted her eyes and looked into the darkened cave.

When Boo thought she heard something she plastered herself to the wall and froze to the spot. She heard a gunshot. It got her moving, the shots were to her right.

Boo could hardly see the entranceway into the cave. She thought she saw shadows moving everywhere in the dim light. She could see the flash from the guns being fired. They lit up the cave's entranceway.

Boo slowly made her way towards the entrance being careful to stay low. She looked up and found herself behind Cruella who was so involved with trying to kill someone that she never noticed her. Boo moved behind a large rock and stayed hidden.

"Chan Dana, you can't win." Jackson yelled. "You need to come out, give yourself up. The League of Law Enforcement has everyone looking for you. There's nowhere to go but back to our time."

Chan Dana's answer was around of bullets fired in Jackson's direction. He quickly ducked and pulled Dude down next to him.

"Stay down, Dude. She will kill you if she gets the chance."

"Moose was directly across from him and asked, "where's Boo?"

"I don't know, but were at a disadvantage here. We can't really see her in the shadows. We've got the light at our backs. She definitely knows where we are."

Dude looked back at the entranceway and said, "maybe we should wait until after dark."

"We can't, because if Boo is still alive....."

Jackson turned to Bill. "We have to be extra careful because she will use the child as a shield, but Bill, we just don't know if she still alive. I'm really sorry."

"We have to assume that she is. Jackson she's a nine-year-old child."

"I still think we have a better chance after dark." Dude said again."

While they were discussing the next move, Chan Dana was on the move. She had a lot of protection from the rocks around her and was going to a higher location. There was a place where the cave turned and a large jagged rock partially closed the entranceway. It offered a perfect blind spot. She could see them, but they wouldn't be able to see her. All she has to do was wait for them to come to her.

Chan Dana left everything behind except her extra ammunition and one of the flashlights. She could come back for the rest later. She took the flashlight and wrapped it with the extra shirt Boo had taken in case it was colder in the cave. It muffled the light so it was dull and less likely to be seen, but it still gave off enough light for her to maneuver in the dim cave.

Boo watched Chan Dana as she moved over to the right, stood up, and began walking towards the jut out where she would wait for Jackson. After she was a distance away, Boo went over to the items Cruella had left behind.

She was quiet when she went through what was left. She picked up a smaller flashlight that had a weaker beam than the one that Cruella carried. Boo took out her handkerchief and wrapped around the top of the flashlight. She switched it on and pointed it at everything Cruella had left behind. To her surprise she found a small twenty-two caliber pistol. It was a six shot. She was familiar with all types of guns because Charlie had many of them. He also felt for her safety she needed to learn how to properly handle and respect a weapon.

Boo was glad that she had paid attention to her brother's instructions. She had no fear of the weapon, only of what type of destruction it could do. Charlie had said sometimes there was no choice.

Boo followed behind Cruella being careful not to make any noise at all. She could still hear the waterfall in the distance and that helped to muffle her footsteps. She could feel the sweat falling from her forehead, but didn't know if it was because she was afraid or because she was running a fever. She felt awful, but didn't have time to deal with that.

Jackson and Bill decided to split up. Dude would go with Jackson. Jackson handed him a gun.

"Do you know how to use this?"

"I do. I hunted a lot."

"I don't want any heroics, you need to stay with me and do everything I tell you to do, when I tell you to do it. Do you understand?"

"Perfectly."

"Jackson I'm going to swing around to the right, you and Dude go left. Call out if you see her."

"Good luck, Bill. Don't forget that she will kill you on site. The woman is vicious, cruel beyond words, and you can't trust anything that she says to you because it will be all lies. Always remember how deadly she is, don't give her the opportunity to shoot you."

Jackson and Bill separated each going in a different direction. Jackson didn't know that he and Dude were actually moving away from Chan Dana's location while Bill was heading straight towards her.

Moose slowly made his way further into the cave, it was getting more difficult to see, but he took advantage of the staggering rock formations that offered him protection. He stopped several times to listen, but could only hear the distant waterfall as it hit the cave floor and ran back down into the river. He inched forward always aware of the danger that could be right around the corner.

Chan Dana was waiting patiently; she knew they would have to come this way to continue into the cave. As far she could see there was no other way in. It was the way in, and the way out, almost like an inviting gateway to the rest of the cave. She made herself as comfortable as possible while she waited hoping that it would be Jackson she saw first.

Boo edged up close to where Cruella was waiting. She was actually on the other side of the river at the shallow end. She looked down and thought she could walk right across if she had to. She was standing between two large rocks that reached upward toward the cave ceiling. She could see Cruella, but was pretty sure that she couldn't see her.

Boo stood far enough back that she would be out of sight. She looked at the pistol in her hands. She decided that she would give it to Jackson so he could defend himself.

Boo looked, and then looked again because she couldn't believe what she was seeing. She rubbed her eyes and peered into the dark cave again. She didn't understand. She grinned, Moose was moving toward them, but that meant he was also moving into Cruella's trap.

Moose. Her Moose, he wasn't dead after all. Cruella didn't kill him that day. Somehow, he was still alive. She had to warn him before it was too late.

Boo glanced over at Cruella, she was crouched behind the rock across from her, waiting. She couldn't let Cruella kill Moose again, she had to do something.

Boo screamed as loud as she could. "Moose, go back, it's a trap."

Cruella jumped out from behind the rock and sprayed several shots at Moose. Moose returned her fire. For several seconds the caverns of the cave resounded with the gunshots. Boo found it deafening.

Boo raised the pistol in her hands, she only had several seconds to make a decision and took careful aim, just like Charlie had showed her. She didn't know if she could pull the trigger until Colella turned to her and shot at her. Boo closed her eyes, pulled the trigger on her pistol, and fell to the ground.

Moose saw Boo fall and rushed over to Chan Dana. He kicked the gun out of her reach and then bent down to check to see if she was alive. There was no pulse. He immediately disregarded her and ran over to where Boo was lying on the ground. He went down to his knees and turn Boo over and into his arms. He pulled the little girl to him and sat down rocking her. He moaned.

"I'm sorry, Bill." Jackson said. "I'm so sorry we couldn't save her."

"Boo grunted and said, "Moose, you're crushing me."

"What? Boo."

"Yeah, it's me." Boo turned and hugged Moose. "I'm so glad you're not dead."

"Right back at you."

"I'm not dead, but my head is killing me, it hurts so bad. I think I have a fever. Moose, did I kill Cruella?"

"Who's Cruella?"

Boo pointed over to Chan Dana. "Her."

"No, sweetheart. You didn't, I did it."

"Can we go home?"

Moose carried Boo out of the cave. When he got a good look at her, he knew that she needed medical care. She had a black eye, her wrists were both raw, and her hand was oozing blood. He could feel the heat in her.

Dude looked at Boo, "we need to take her to an emergency room."

"No, I want to go home. Moose, Dillon can fix me."

Moose handed Boo over to Dude and walked over to Jackson. "Can you take care of this mess?"

Jackson knew exactly what Bill was talking about. He would stay behind and make sure that everything disappeared and the people of this time would never be aware of what happened here today. He is very good at that and it wouldn't be the first time that is clean up a mess.

"I'll take care of everything. You take the little one home; I'll meet you back in our time."

The two men shook hands. Boo grinned over a Jackson. "Are you Jackson?"

He went over to her and gently touched her cheek, "I am Jackson."

"Cruella wanted to kill you. I tried to warn you, but I don't know if you heard me."

Thank you for the warning. It probably saved my life."

"Did you save my Moose?"

"I guess you could say that."

"That's good because he is so worth saving. I love my Moose."

"He gently touched her cheek again. "You need to rest and get well."

"First, I have to call Charlie."

Chapter 29

Dude examined Boo's wrists carefully. He went into the pharmacy and bought some bandages, antibiotic ointment, and ibuprofen. They drove back to the motel where Dude washed Boo's wrists before applying antibiotic. He loosely wrapped her wrists in gauze and gave her to ibuprofen with a glass of water.

"Thanks, Dude. It feels better already."

"The ibuprofen should help with the fever. Once that goes down, you'll be feeling much better."

"You did a really good job. Can I call Charlie now"

Moose sat down and pulled Boo onto his lap. "Boo, you know I'm from another time, and Chan Dana was also from that time. This is something you can't tell anyone about."

"She was bad. Evil. That's why I called her Cruella."

"I know. She was evil in our time too. She killed a lot of good people."

"But she's gone now and can't hurt anyone again."

"You're right, when you talk to Charlie you just need to tell him that she got way."

"But she's dead."

"Jackson is going to take Chan Dana back to our time. She never belonged here."

"Charlie knows that you're from the future."

"That's also something we have to keep between all of us. Do you think you understand?"

"Maybe, I guess. I just won't say anything."

~~~

When they drove up to the ranch Charlie and Brandon were waiting for them, but it was Connery who jumped into the car and proceeded to give Boo a once over. She hugged the dog to her.

Charlie grabbed Boo and hugged her tightly to him, he kissed both of her cheeks. "I've missed you, Charlie, really bad."

Brandon also got it into the act, he hugged Boo and laughed, "boy, it's never been so quiet around here."

"I missed you too, Brandon."

Dillon frowned at Boo. He pulled her into his embrace and held her. "I've never been so scared. Don't ever do that again. I need to take care of your injuries, but right now, you need to go to bed and stay there."

"I do feel kind of crummy."

Dillon took her hand into his. "That is because your hand is infected so you'll have to be on antibiotics for a while. We also have to get your fever down. Boo, do you need to talk about what happened?"

"I can't tell you any more than I did. Most of the time she kept me tied up in a motel room. I don't remember much."

"And then she just released you in Bowling Green, Kentucky?"

"Pretty much. She thought I was too much trouble."

Dillon leaned over and kissed her cheek again. "Actually, I can understand that."
~~~

They would never resolve the mystery of Chan Dana Ray, or truly understand why she took Boo. That was a secret that Boo would always keep to herself. Chan Dana would never be found by the authorities. After a while it was considered a cold case.

Chapter 30

It had been over two weeks and Boo felt much better, she would go back to school on Monday. She spoke to the Sheriff and he accepted her story. There was a search for Chan Dana, but Boo knew that they would never find her.

Jackson had covered up everything and transported her body back to the future. Boo didn't know what would happen there, but Moose assured her that everything would be taking care of and he would not be sent to jail for killing Chan Dana. She had worried about that.

What Boo didn't know was that it was her bullet that had killed Chan Dana. She had hit her just right of the heart. She died instantly. Boo had saved Moose's life when Chan Dana zeroed in on him, it was a split second that made the difference.

Moose would never reveal that Boo had killed Chan Dana. She was a child, and he would not leave her with that memory. In the end it didn't matter who had killed her. She was insane just like her father, and now they were both gone, dead. It was time to rebuild the earth of the future. He wanted his daughter, Kara, to know what a dog was, to hold it and have one as a friend. This was just one of the things he intended to change.

Moose decided that he would take back some of the most important things they would need to rebuild. He wanted to see farms like they had here. Farms with horses, cattle, lambs, and the cow. They would definitely need cows. He had gotten a real taste for milk.

Moose was sitting on the front porch scratching Connery's ears when Boo sat down next to him and handed him a root beer

"Connery's going to miss you."

Moose turned to Boo. "Not as much as I'm going to miss you."

Boo took Moose's hand in hers. "Don't go. Stay with us."

"I can't. I have another life that I have to go back to."

"You can have a life here with us."

Moose took a picture out of his pocket and handed it to Boo she studied the picture carefully, turn to him and asked, "who is she?" and then she whispered, "she looks like me."

"She looks enough like you to be your sister. She's my daughter, Kara."

"I didn't know you had a daughter. You never said. "How come we look so much alike?"

Moose smiled. "It's complicated, but I'll try to explain a little bit of it to. My daughter is actually related to you. You are her great, great, great, well it's a lot of greats, but the bottom line is that your family and mine are linked. Somewhere down the line we've been intertwined."

"So, you're saying were some kind of kin?"

"We are."

Boo looked at the picture again. "Wait here."

Boo ran upstairs to her bedroom, opened the dresser drawer and pulled out a small box. She found her old school pictures, took one out and went back downstairs.

Boo handed the picture to Moose. He compared the two pictures. It was remarkable, they could've been twins.

"Do you have to leave?"

Moose grinned at Boo. "I'm afraid so. This isn't my time and I miss my daughter. I've been gone for a long time. I have to go back to my time and make it productive again. It's going to take a long time to rebuild what Chan Dana and her father destroyed. I want to be a part of the rebuilding of earth. There's so much to do. I am going to bring seeds back from your time to help my world.

I want my people to know what a horse is, and dogs like Connery. There's so much to do, but now that the evil is gone, I am sure it will happen."

"Chan Dana Ray, she was really evil."

"Yes, her and her father."

Boo hug Moose to her. "I'll miss you so much. Can you come back and visit me again?"

"I don't know. These things are decided by the League of Law Enforcement. There has to be approvals and......"

Moose knew by Boo's confused look that she wasn't understanding about the League and even if he tried to explain it to her, she wouldn't understand. He decided to make it simple.

"If I can, I will come back to see you. I will never forget you, Boo."

"When do you have to go?"

"Tomorrow."

Boo and Moose spent the evening together. They watch the sunset in the western sky as it went down. It made Boo cry.

Moose waited until the entire household was asleep before he left. Connery followed him out to the barn. Moose leaned down to pet the dog.

"You need to go back to Boo. You can't go with me. He watched as Connery turned around and headed back for the ranch house. He would miss all of them, but he would never forget them. He would take trips back to this time because he wanted the best for his world and he needed things that he could acquire here.

"I'll probably need to make a lot of trips back."

Moose felt the blue stone in his pocket. He pulled it out and held it in his hand. "Thank you, Boo."

Moose got out his transporter and activated it.

MORE BOOKS BY:

J.W. BECKER

The Flow River Series:

Returning to Flow River and Murder

Hannah's Secret

Greed, Money, and Murder

Murder at 3 P.M.

The Death of Travis McKenna

Deadly Lies   True Intent

A Time of Waiting

The Forever Series:

Book #1   Dust, Bones, and the Forever

Book #2   Journey toward the Forever

Book #3   Running into the Forever

Book #4   Dead Is Forever

Book #5   Returned to Evil

Ghost Stories:

Murder of a Ghost

Murder of a Blue Lady

Westerns:

The Captives: The Story of Wasser Thomas

Trail of Destiny: The Joseph Lansing Story

Comanche: The Martin McCoy Story

Single Books:

Time to Play the Game and Count the Dead

Shadows from the past

The Truth Is Always at an Angle

Step into Darkness

Shadows in the Darkness

Something Evil Follows

1918 When the World Shook with Fear

Good Child Bad Child Wrong Child

Children's Books:

Welcome to Halloween

Christmas: A Special Time of Year

Stories from My Childhood

The Missing Angel

The Santa Letter

The Santa Sack

The Santa Sleigh

To the readers of my Books:

I would like to thank you for reading my Books. To me each one of these Books represents something special, they are a part of me. I hope that everyone who has taken the time to walk through these Books, enjoys them as much as I did when I wrote them.

You can only start an adventure with the first word written. Enjoy everything you read because whether you realize it or not, it is always a learning experience. Sit back and enjoy your time in someone else's world.

With my warmest regards,

J. W. Becker